# Your Free Gift

I wanted to show my appreciation for
supporting my work so I've put
together a Bonus Chapter for you,

(But don't read it until you've finished this book).

Just visit the link below:

http://outerbanks1_freegift.gr8.com/

Thanks!

Phoebe T. Eggli

Timber Publishing

# A PINCH OF SEA SALT AND A DASH OF MURDER

## PHOEBE T. EGGLI

Dedicated to my supportive friends and family.

Life delivers punches along the way,

But I'm grateful for the amazing people in my life

Who've helped me get back up; who believe in me.

May you also have similar people in your life;

And be one as well!

# Table of Contents

# Chapter 1

Melissa awoke this morning much like every morning in the last four years – long before the sun peeked over the Atlantic Ocean. No alarm clock was needed. She hadn't always been a morning person. Even throughout her twenty year marriage to a test pilot who was up and out the door before 4:30 every morning, she had always gone back to bed as soon as he kissed her goodbye for the day – at least for an hour or two. Since his death four years prior in a tragic plane crash of an experimental Cessna Citation X jet, her eyes would open of their own accord almost to the minute Kevin would've been softly planting a kiss on her lips. Sometimes she imagined she still felt his kiss and would waken with a smile. This was such a morning.

Tiptoeing through the hallway so as not to awaken her nephew Logan snoring in the guest room, Melissa began her day by starting the coffee pot to brewing – the strongest blend she could find at the local corner market. Breakfast, for her at least, consisted of cut-up apples, bananas, and cantaloupe. With Logan here for the summer, there was only one way to wake him up – the smell of turkey bacon being nuked in the microwave. Surely the newly crowned teenager would prefer to sleep the day away, so she decided to wait another hour before disturbing his slumber.

Melissa's brother John David and his wife had sent the boy to her every summer since an early age. Following her husband Kevin's death, they used the excuse that he was to keep her company so she wouldn't be so lonely all the time. They also said Logan needed to learn responsibility by helping her out with the bakery. Logan had a different opinion – they wanted to get rid of him for the summer so they wouldn't have to take time away from their hectic careers to take care of him. Sadly, his take on the situation was closer to the truth.

Regardless, he was incredibly helpful in the bakery and had even shown an interest in learning to bake sweets such as pastries and tea cakes since he was little. He wasn't really enthused about his Aunt Mel's specialty – artisan breads. What teenage boy would be? She tried to minimize his time at the bakery so he could still enjoy being at the beach for the summer. Logan loved fishing off the municipal pier for hours on end and had even tried surfing last summer. He hadn't been successful in the latter activity, but at least he wasn't afraid to try. It was better than having the boy sitting in front of a television playing Xbox all day long, which would've been his fate if he stayed in Charlotte with his folks.

Without children of her own, not for a lack of trying for many years and throwing money down the infertility treatment route, summers spent caring for Logan were a real blessing. At 44 years of age, and now single, Melissa had resigned herself to never becoming a mom herself.

Melissa filled her coffee mug and went to enjoy the last remnants of the darkness and watch the sunrise from the second-story wooden deck. This was her favorite time of day, before the crazy hustle bustle of operating her own bakery in town, the "Kill Devil Delicacies". When she moved back to her hometown four years ago she took the miniscule amount she had in savings and the proceeds from her husband's life insurance policy to open her own bakery, which had always been her dream. Melissa liked to think her bakery was unique in that she didn't create traditional birthday cakes and cupcakes. Her specialty was artisan breads and hers was the only shop in town that provided them. There were two other bakeries in town. One, owned by her Italian friend Maria and her husband Antonio, cornered the traditional sweets market such as cakes, cupcakes, pies, and donuts.

The other bakery was owned by her long-time rival since high school, Linda Stevenson who designed and created the most gorgeous and unique wedding cakes to be found anywhere on the North Carolina coastline. Her business was called "Heavenly

Creations". Melissa had thought, wrongly, that when she came back to town things would be different with Linda. For whatever reason it seemed Linda was not going to let jealousies and misunderstandings from high school simply go. Every once in a while, like this particular morning, she would attempt to puzzle out why Linda still treated her with hostility. Realizing it was a lost cause, Melissa sighed and finished her first cup of coffee. With the sun starting to peer out from the horizon she knew it was time to wake Logan with the scrumptious smells of his breakfast.

After feeding the bottomless pit that was Logan's stomach, she kissed him on the top of his dusky brown head – something he acted as if offended his teenage boy tendencies but secretly he relished – and finished getting ready for work. A few minutes later, with her light auburn hair tied up in a ponytail for the day, they were both out the door and ready to enjoy the day. The weatherman had called for clear skies all week and temperatures in the low 90s. Despite the sun being up for just a short while, the humidity had already set in and beads of perspiration sprung up on their foreheads as they walked the seven blocks from Melissa's beachside cottage to the bakery.

On their walk they passed other locals starting their day. A few dedicated runners – Melissa had tried running when she was younger but her shin splints kept her to a brisk walk these days – and other shop owners readying for the first official week of the summer tourist season. It wasn't until the duo rounded the corner to enter the back entrance of the single story building that housed the bakery that Melissa noticed something was wrong. The grey heavy metal door was slightly ajar. Upon closer inspection she could see where the lock had been jimmied. Her first thought was the shop had been robbed. Being a small town, crime was a rare event but tourist season seemed to bring in a bit more than the usual. "Great," Melissa thought, "first week and we're already having issues! Should be fun summer!"

Logan took things into his own hands and before Melissa could stop him, he threw open the door and ran inside with his aunt close on his heels. Her initial concern was the crooks were still in the shop and could hurt her nephew. She was not prepared for the sight that she beheld. Logan had stopped right inside the door and was frozen in place. It only took a moment for her to take in the situation and forcibly turn him away from the scene. Pulling him back out of the building, he turned towards the dumpster and hurled his turkey bacon and clementine breakfast back up. Melissa was torn between kneeling beside him and running back into the shop. With shaky hands, she dialed 911 from her cell phone as she walked back in to see if there was anything she could do for the bloodied body lying perfectly still on the floor of her bakery.

# Chapter 2

A couple hours later, Melissa and Logan were seated in the town's tiny police department waiting area. The paramedics had shown up at the bakery within a few minutes of her call and had taken the dead body of her greatest competitor, Linda Stevenson, away to the county morgue. The entire block had been cordoned off by the police as they investigated the crime scene. Two officers had initially checked that Melissa and her nephew were okay. Later the same two officers escorted them to the department's headquarters for questioning. Jason Payne, the younger but still approaching middle age detective, had reassured Melissa it was just procedure. Since they had found the body, the police needed their statements. However, his older and stouter partner Larry Reynolds, had cast more than one suspicious glance in her direction during the short ride over.

Sipping tepid water from a paper cup, Melissa couldn't make sense of anything and she was worried about Logan's emotional state. Finding a dead body was frightening for anyone but she imagined more so for a young impressionable teenage boy. Questions raced through her mind: What happened to Linda? How did she end up in her shop? Why was she in her shop? Who would want to hurt her competitor and why do so in the Kill Devil Delicacies bakery? Nothing about this situation made any sense.

Melissa had known Linda since elementary school. They had been good friends until junior year of high school. They both loved cooking and planned to attend culinary school after graduation. Their friendship became strained when the hot shot jock quarterback Brian Webber asked Melissa out on a movie date. She wasn't aware until later that Linda was crushing on the big guy. By that time, the damage was done and Melissa was equally infatuated with him. She was unable to step aside to give her taller, leggier blonde friend a chance with him and Linda was unable to forgive her. The friendship had declined rapidly from that point. The situation was only made worse when the following year Melissa won the coveted title of Homecoming Queen. Twenty-something years later when she returned to Kill Devil Hills a widow, their friendship had still not recovered. Melissa remembered the day Linda found out she was opening her own bakery just a couple blocks away from her own. The now somewhat plump box-colored platinum blonde had exploded in a tantrum unsuitable for a five year old, much less a 40 year old woman.

None of that mattered now, of course. Melissa questioned why it had ever mattered. Her thoughts turned to all the times she could've reached out to reconcile with Linda. She hadn't done so. The other woman had been so spiteful when Melissa returned to town. She had made not very well veiled comments about how it served her rival justly to not have children since she didn't have a real heart anyway. There had been other gossip, she suspected originating from Linda, which had been hurtful. Reeling from the death of her husband, Melissa had simply written off any reconciliation with her former friend as not being worth the effort. Regretfully, it was too late now.

It didn't take long for the police to get around to questioning them. Melissa watched with concern as they led Logan away to an interview room alone. The tall one, Detective Payne, reassured her that they had waited so long because they couldn't question a minor until a social services representative arrived. "Terrific," Melissa thought with even more anxiety, "my brother sends his only child to me for the summer for safe keeping and now the boy needs social services and probably a shrink!"

She wasn't left waiting long for her turn. The older, rounder in the middle, detective ushered her to another interview room. He gruffly told her to take a seat and he would be right back. Melissa assumed he was going to the adjoining room to consult with whoever was observing behind the two-way mirror before questioning her. She had watched enough "Law and Order" and "Castle" to know there was always someone behind the mirror. The question in her mind was "Why am I being treated like a suspect?" She had simply been the one to find Linda's body. Her uneasiness grew the longer the detective held off coming back into the room.

A few minutes later the door opened and both detectives entered the room. By the expressions on their faces Melissa guessed it was time to play Good Cop/Bad Cop. The tall, muscular looking man with a short, military-style crew cut and kind brown eyes was Detective Jason Payne. He carried in two Styrofoam cups of coffee and set one down in front of her. The older, barrel-chested gentleman was Detective Larry Reynolds. He plopped down in the metal chair directly across from her with a scowl. "Yes," she thought, "this is more than taking my statement. This is an interrogation."

Thankfully Detective Payne began by kindly asking how she was holding up under the ordeal and commiserating that it must have been awful to find the body. Bad cop chimed in, "Yeah, in your own shop. Not hers," with emphasis on the word "your". Detective Payne gave his partner a sideways warning glance as if to check the old man's enthusiasm to convict before even getting the facts. Melissa couldn't help thinking they were professionals at the good cop/bad cop game.

The interview proceeded with "good cop" asking most the questions and the "bad cop" jotting down notes along with scowling at her. He even rolled his eyes a couple of times as if he did not believe a word she said. After the drama of the morning, Melissa's emotional state was under duress and this guy was not helping.

She answered every question the best she could and repeated her story at least five times. She and her nephew had left her house that morning to go to work at her bakery. They walked there – approximately seven blocks. Didn't see anything out of the ordinary until they reached the back of the building housing her shop. The door was slightly ajar and it looked as if the lock had been tampered with. Logan was the first to enter the building with her closely on his heels where they found Linda in a pool of blood on the floor midway between the counter housing the cooling racks and the back door. No, she had no idea why Linda would be in her shop or how she got in. No, Linda did not have a key to the Kill Devil Delicacies bakery. Yes, Melissa knew Linda ever since high school. Yes, she and Linda were indirect competitors since Melissa specialized in breads and French pastries while Linda was the queen of wedding cakes. She couldn't recall the last time she saw Linda alive. They didn't cross paths too often.

Detective "Grumpy" jumped on the idea that despite being in the same business in a very small town that the two ladies seemed to stay out of each other's orbits. He leaned his head on his hands as he stared intently at her as if waiting for her to cave with some earth-shattering confession. Despite warning glances from his partner, he continued his line of questioning. Detective "Soft Brown Eyes" gave Melissa an apologetic look.

An hour and a half later, with Melissa's patience worn thin by the aggravating detective, she turned to Detective Payne to ask if someone could please check on her nephew as she was worried about the boy. Surprisingly, he asked his partner to fulfill the request and stayed with her. As the door shut behind the other cop, he leaned back in the metal chair that creaked under the weight of his 6'3" frame. "Mrs. Maples, please accept my apologies for my partner's manners, or lack thereof. I know you must be exhausted after this entire ordeal. Larry's just anxious to wrap up his last case before retirement. He means well, really."

Perturbed, Melissa replied, "Well, I hope he's not planning on pinning this on an innocent person just so he can get his retirement watch from the department and go fishing." The last thing she needed was an overzealous cop with his eye on the door instead of the evidence. Detective Payne attempted to reassure her that was not the case at all, but she still had doubts as the older man re-entered the room.

"Your nephew is fine. He's watching television in the main lobby. The social worker has called his parents to notify them of the situation." He appeared down right gleeful that she had been ratted out to her own brother by the social worker instead of giving her a chance to explain what had happened. John David would probably understand she hadn't "intended" to subject his son to the dramatic sight of a dead body, but she also knew his wife, Kathleen, would be livid.

Taking a deep breath, Melissa looked the detective in the eye and asked if there was anything else they needed from her. If not, she needed to take Logan home to see to his needs. She had answered their questions over and over. Going over it again would not add anything to the case since that really was everything she knew. Sensing her frustration, Detective Payne apologized again and agreed they had all the information they needed from her. His partner added the caveat, "If you DO remember anything else, please contact us immediately." She agreed and was allowed to leave the interview room. Finding Logan with eyes glossed over staring at the overhead television set showing reruns of "Fresh

Prince of Bel Air", Melissa took his hand and they walked out the precinct doors and towards home.

## Chapter 3

Waiting on the wooden steps outside Melissa's cottage was a petite young woman with strawberry blonde hair hanging down to the small of her back. Britney Williams was her assistant at the bakery. Britney had gorgeous, long flowing strawberry blonde hair and a flawless complexion that was the envy of every woman, young and old, in town. Dressed in her usual work attire – Capri pants and a tight, white cropped t-shirt – Melissa could read the concern in her face. The young woman was trying to hold it together but it was clear by the tears threatening to overflow her sky blue eyes that she was about to lose that fight.

Melissa, trying to remain calm herself, invited Britney inside the house and sent Logan to get a shower and rest a while in his room. He hadn't said much on the walk home which worried her. Hopefully after they both had time to process the day's events individually, they could console each other. Watching the young man retreat to his small bedroom at the back of the house, Melissa let out a long sigh and turned to her assistant.

She thought she was doing a good job of holding it together, but caught her hands shaking as she put water on to boil for some soothing herbal tea. Melissa was more of a coffee drinker, but circumstances being what they were, she doubted the need for more caffeine. Britney immediately began barraging her with rapid fire questions about what had happened and explaining her shock at showing up for work expecting to be chastised for being late yet again but instead finding the place cordoned off by police tape. Not wanting Logan to hear her retelling the story so as not to upset him even more, Melissa gave Britney the "shush" sign by placing her finger over her lips and motioning for her to join her on the deck.

Taking a few sips of her hot chamomile tea, Melissa filled Britney in on the events as they had transpired that morning – finding the back door to the shop open, finding the dead body of Linda Stevenson inside, and the hostile police interrogation. Shock was apparent on the young woman's face. After taking some moments to compile her thoughts, Britney burst out, "Well, that's just ridiculous! Why would they treat you like that? You didn't kill her!" Melissa didn't allow her to continue ranting for fear Logan would hear.

In a softer tone, Britney speculated who would want to murder Linda. Sure, she wasn't the nicest lady in town and had gone out of her way to be spiteful towards Melissa when she came back to Kill Devil Hills, but that didn't seem to make her a target for murder. The young woman seemed more alarmed that the cops had kept Melissa for questioning so long, than the actual fact that a woman had been found dead in the bakery.

Although Melissa didn't think it would do any good, Britney insisted on talking to her boyfriend, Eddie (Edward Johnson, III to be exact) to get his daddy – billionaire shipping magnate and top dog all along the North Carolina coast – to set the police department straight. While appreciating the gesture, Melissa knew it would probably do more harm than good to have the elder Mr. Johnson make a call on her behalf.

She was saved from more of Britney's broad declarations of getting the cops off her back when the doorbell rang announcing another guest. Not really excited about hosting a small gathering, when she just wanted to crawl back in bed and pretend this day had not happened, she reluctantly answered the door. Luckily, it was her good friend Cheryl who owned the one and only soup and salad restaurant immediately across from the Kill Devil Delicacies. Cheryl had been Melissa's best customer since opening day by ordering daily deliveries of breadsticks and artisan bread loaves to serve with her soups and salads. They both volunteered at the local soup kitchen twice a week and provided Meals-on-Wheels as well. Their friendship had blossomed over the last couple of years. Cheryl, and their other friend Maria whose husband owned the other bakery in town, insisted that Melissa get out at least once a month for a girls' night. At first she had resisted, but Cheryl wouldn't allow her to sit at home by herself every night watching crime dramas or reality television. Her pestering finally worked and now Melissa looked forward to their nights out on the town. Today especially, she could use her friend's support. At least she could count on Cheryl not to become hysterical which was close to what Britney was doing.

Seeing the frustration in Melissa's eyes, Cheryl took charge of the situation. After a few more minutes, she had somehow convinced Britney that she should go in order for her weary boss to rest after her ordeal. Even as she was nearly shoved out the door by Cheryl, Britney continued proclaiming that she would tell the cops what was what and warn them to leave her friend alone. As the door shut behind her, both women rolled their eyes at the younger woman's dramatics and let out simultaneous sighs of exasperation. There had been many times throughout their acquaintance that Cheryl had asked her, "How do you deal with that little tart?"

Checking on Logan, who had fallen asleep with his feet dangling off the edge of the bed and his hair still damp, Melissa kissed him softly on the forehead and pulled the covers over his lankly teenage body. She returned to the kitchen to find Cheryl warming up some of her famous bacon and cheddar potato soup on the stove. "Figured you could use some comfort food," she ordered Melissa to take a seat and relax.

"Don't think I will be relaxing anytime soon. Actually, what I really need to do is call my brother to let him know how Logan is holding up. Would you mind…" but before she could finish her question, Cheryl shooed her out of the kitchen to make her call. John David was concerned about them both. Surprisingly, he didn't insist on driving out to pick up Logan and haul him back to Charlotte for the remainder of the summer but rather wanted him to remain there to support her. Part of her thought it was a sweet gesture, but the other part wondered if it had more to do with not wanting to be burdened with the drive and having to deal with a rambunctious teenage for the next three months. After years of desperately trying to have a child with her late husband and being disappointed, Melissa could never understand how her own brother and sister-in-law so nonchalantly cast their one and only child aside while they furiously focused on their high-profile banking careers.

Not feeling much better after her conversation with Logan's father, Melissa returned to the kitchen to find Cheryl had ladled out the scrumptious soup into whole wheat bread bowls and had replaced Melissa's cup of tea with a glass of red wine. "Thought you could use something a teeny bit stronger," she quipped with a small grin. The two ladies sat at the table silently enjoying their soup.

It wasn't until the soup was gone and Melissa was picking off bits of bread that she opened up to Cheryl about her experiences that day. She assumed someone had contacted Linda's family. Her two children, Andrea and Charles (aka Chuck) were living in Atlanta and New York, respectively. Her husband was out of town at a teacher's convention in Raleigh but was on his way back. The locals were gossiping and speculating about what had happened but no one seemed to know why Linda Stevenson had been in Melissa's bakery or how the pleasantly plump, platinum blonde ended up dead. The cops had not yet released any information, but Cheryl expected there would be something on the evening news at least.

More relaxed now, Melissa and Cheryl continued their conversation out on the deck. A couple hours later, Logan made an appearance with his disheveled hair covering his eyes. His aunt knew without lifting the hair away that the boy's eyes were red and swollen from crying. He was trying to give off the "I'm a big boy and can handle anything" vibe but wasn't fooling anyone. Cheryl jumped up to fetch some soup for the young man. He ate the meal with gusto. Despite the morning's events, there was no holding back a teenage boy's appetite; Logan had no trouble packing away the food. Not to mention it was Cheryl's special recipe.

Realizing the two needed their space, Cheryl made an excuse and left a little while later. At first, the aunt and nephew sat quietly out on the deck in their over-sized Adirondack chairs. Melissa was the first to break the silence by explaining that she had contacted his father. Logan didn't seem surprised his parents intended to leave him there. Actually, he was glad. He loved his Aunt Mel dearly. Every summer she made him feel more loved and cared for than he ever felt when with his parents. He certainly didn't wish to leave her now.

Not wanting to worry him, Melissa tried to steer the conversation away from Linda's unfortunate demise. A few failed attempts later, they agreed to move inside and veg out in front of the television together. The sun was starting to set, but the little time spent outside had left Logan's fair skin pinker than before and his nose more freckled. Besides, the mosquitos were relentless this time of year. They were both scratching at bites as they made their way inside.

Clicking the remote to turn on the 32 inch flat screen television she had purchased a few months back, they settled in their respective spots – hers in the oversized, well-worn chair with her feet curled underneath her and his on the matching sofa. Deciding against their usual crime drama series, Melissa sought something with a lighter fare, perhaps a comedy sitcom. Unfortunately, the chosen show was interrupted by a local news special report live from Kill Devil Hills, NC.

A smiling and attractive young woman from the local news station was broadcasting live from in front of Melissa's bakery. "This is Sonya Patterson from News Channel 12 reporting from the scene of a gruesome murder in the quiet seaside town of Kill Devil Hills. Channel 12 has learned that the shop just behind me is a bakery owned by Melissa Jones Maples and is where her competitor Linda Patterson was found dead this morning. Local residents are shocked. The police took Mrs. Maples and her nephew into custody this morning for questioning when they responded to a 911 call. Both were later released." Video footage showed Melissa and Logan being ushered to a waiting police car. It did indeed look like they were being "taken into custody".

The reporter continued, "Police have not released details of the murder or discussed any evidence that was obtained from the scene. However, this reporter spoke briefly with the husband of the victim this afternoon." A picture appeared on the screen of Mr. Stevenson as well as a telephone icon. The recording played was of a distraught husband in shock but

Melissa was shocked at his words. He basically told the reporter that his wife was a saint and had never understood why Mrs. Maples despised her so much. He elaborated that the two had a fierce rivalry since high school, but his wife had tried to patch things up with her when the woman came back to town after her husband's questionable death in an airplane crash a few years back. However, she had been rebuffed and constantly subjected to gossip orchestrated by her rival. In his mind, there was no doubt that Mrs. Maples had something to do with his wife's death.

Shocked and outraged, Melissa tried to turn off the television but in her haste hit the volume button instead of "off". The last thing she and Logan heard was the reporter signing off her broadcast saying, "The police have not commented but it is clear to everyone else in town that it is not a coincidence Mrs. Stevenson was found in the Kill Devil Delicacies bakery. We hope to have more information for our viewers tomorrow when the police chief gives his news conference briefing at 10 AM."

The TV went dark and all was silent. Neither Melissa nor Logan could find their voice to say anything. Apparently, the public had made up their minds that she was to blame for Linda's death. The woman had been found in her shop, after all. However, the malarkey about there being a fierce rivalry and that Linda had tried to be nice to her when she returned to

33

town was ridiculous! Melissa had done her best to simply ignore the woman's unveiled attempts at hostility for years. Frankly, she could've cared less about being in competition with the woman. As she saw it, they each had their own niche of the bakery market, thus there was no professional rivalry. The allusion that Kevin's tragic death in the Cessna experimental aircraft was "questionable" was even more absurd!

With dread she looked over at Logan who had gone ashen white despite his earlier pinkish tinge. Melissa started to say something in an effort to comfort her nephew. Before she could even think of the right words to say, he unexpectedly jumped up. With anger growing in his voice and his hazel eyes flashing with gold flecks, he began to rant about the stupidity of the entire situation. How could anyone believe his Aunt Mel had anything to do with that crazy woman's death?! That reporter should be fired immediately and Mr. Stevenson is obviously in need of a shrink if he believes even half of the bull---- coming out of his mouth! She allowed him to continue to pace the living room and rave about the lack of sense and justice being shown by this little "hick" town.

Listening to her nephew, dread built up in Melissa's mind. If folks really believed she was guilty of killing Linda she was in trouble. Even the detective from earlier today was ready to write her off as the killer so he could waltz over to his retirement party. If the town had already made its mind up against her, and the cops weren't going to do their job and find the real killer, that left her only one option. Find the killer herself, before they locked her up for a crime she did not commit.

## Chapter 4

Although neither slept well, or really at all, that night, Melissa and Logan were both up before the sun. Coffee mugs filled to the brim, they headed out to the bakery before any of the locals were up and about their day. She had tried to convince Logan to stay home that day and not to worry about her, but the young man was on a mission. "No one, and I mean NO ONE, is going to railroad my Aunt Mel!" he had declared. Aunt Mel was grateful he believed so strongly in her, but she didn't want him getting messed up in this craziness. However, if left to his own devices, Logan was more apt to get himself into trouble while "investigating" her case. Not seeing another way out, she decided that keeping him close was probably the best course of action.

Logan had noticed a news van parked on the other side of the house earlier that morning, so they crept out a side door and kept to the shadows until they were well out of sight. They hurried along the seven blocks from the house to the bakery. The more she thought about it, the more Melissa realized she couldn't trust the police to handle the investigation properly. It was a shame she had such little faith in them, especially since the one with the kind brown eyes was somewhat attractive and seemed trustworthy. Well, kind eyes or not, she couldn't count on the cops to save the day. This wasn't "Castle", this was real life. And in real life, the police don't always get their man or woman.

The back of the building was still blocked off with police tape that read "Do Not Cross". However, the front was devoid of the tape so Melissa let herself into her own shop through the front door. The place was dark and smelled of something that was not in line with a bakery. She suspected that stench was Linda's blood but didn't want to say anything to Logan about it. Wouldn't do any good to creep the kid out. She was creeped out enough for them both. The boy moved to turn on the lights but Melissa stopped him. The last thing she wanted was for others to notice the lights and come over to confront her invading a crime scene, even if it was her own store. Instead she used the flashlight app on her phone to see her way around. Truth be told, she knew the place so well she could operate an entire day in the store while blindfolded.

Motioning to Logan to stay behind her and not touch anything, Melissa first inspected the front windows and door to see if anything was amiss. Then she moved around the few tables in the place with the wooden chairs still piled on top from when the bakery had closed two nights earlier. Nothing seemed out of place. The customer counter and display cases showed signs of a white powdery substance she suspected the cops had used to dust for prints. The glass enclosed shelves that normally held breads and pastries were empty and cleaned – not even a crumb. She never served anything that was not made fresh that day. Anything not purchased at the end of the day was delivered to the local soup kitchen. With Logan here for the summer, that was one of his duties.

The cash register had also been dusted for prints. Melissa grabbed a pen in a cup next to the register to punch in the code to open it without leaving any fingerprints. It was empty. All cash was removed nightly and placed in the safe in her back office or taken to the bank night depository. Thinking back, she remembered that Britney had offered to take the deposit bag the evening in question and had offered to close up the shop for Melissa so she could get home early to cook a decent meal for Logan. Despite loving to bake, and having graduated with honors from a culinary program, she was not big on cooking everyday meals. A thorough sweep of the front of the shop revealed nothing out of the ordinary, other than the fingerprint dusting powder that the cops had not cleaned up during their initial investigation.

Beginning to think this was a big mistake to come down to the bakery to check things out on her own, Melissa eyed the back of the store. Knowing that was where the crime occurred so that would be where any evidence had been left, she dreaded walking back there. Even more so, she dreaded what she would find even though the cops had most likely taken anything of significance. Taking a deep breath, she used her hip to push open the door leading to the back of the store.

It was pitch black in this area of the shop. The door to the front obscured all light from the outside and should shield any light from the back of the store from anyone walking past outside. Considering her options, walk around a crime scene using the tiny flashlight app on her phone or risking turning on the lights, Melissa chose the latter. The overhead lights flickered briefly and then hummed on fully.

Too late, she realized Logan probably should've stayed out front. The scene before them was disturbing. Pots and pans and baking utensils had been strewn all over the counters and floors. But the disturbing part was the blood splattered on the corner of the countertop she used for cooling breads fresh from the oven and the blood that had dried into the concrete floor. She doubted bleach was going to get that stain out, ever. The police had left the taped outline of Linda's body as it had been discovered. The blood stain appeared to begin at the head and then flowed in an outward pattern. There were specks of dried blood on the walls as well with a smudge of it caked on the door knob leading to the alleyway behind the store.

Trying not to allow herself to focus on the gory scene that used to be her favorite place in the world. The place where she hummed Bon Jovi songs while making her masterpieces on a daily basis. It was truly the one place where she always felt at home since Kevin died. Melissa doubted she would ever feel that way again. At least, not here.

Logan reached over to pick something up off the floor, but Melissa stopped him. If it had any value as evidence, she was sure the police would've bagged it and taken it away, but just in case she didn't want to contaminate the crime scene. Instead she used her phone to snap a few pictures. Looking around, there didn't seem a lot that could be useful, but being an amateur investigator Melissa was afraid to overlook anything so she took pictures of everything.

After what she considered a thorough inspection of the back work area, Melissa moved to access her office. Using her shirt to cover her hand as she tried the knob, she was surprised to find her office was unlocked. She never left the shop without locking the office. After working for catering companies in Greensboro while Kevin pursued flying, she had learned that the number one way to protect your valuables, especially clients' information and special recipes, was to keep everything locked in a safe that was locked behind a fake wall that was hidden behind a bookcase or picture that was in a locked office. Not just a simple push button or click lock found on most home or office doors. No, it had to be a cipher lock and the code must be changed every week if not more often. Melissa had even considered a digital lock that would only open after finger print scan but talked herself out of it. No, this office had been locked when she left the other night. Now it wasn't. The question was…did the cops unlock the door somehow or did Linda or her killer unlock it?

Again, that question kept popping back up…Why was Linda in HER bakery? Melissa didn't have time to dwell on that as moments later they heard the sound of the front door to the bakery opening.

Melissa motioned for Logan to get behind her. A lot of good that would do since he was almost as tall as she was. By next summer he would tower over his aunt. The light switch was too far away for her to reach to turn off so she grabbed his hand and moved them behind the office door as quietly as she could without alerting whoever may be around. Footsteps could be heard as whoever was inside the shop with them made their way around the front counter and through the swinging half-door to the area behind the counter. Melissa couldn't recall if she'd closed the cash register. If it was an intruder wishing to rob them, perhaps once they saw the empty register, hopefully they would simply leave.

Light footsteps continued towards the door leading to the back work area. When she heard the door swing open, Melissa pushed on the office door hoping to keep it shut in case the intruder tried to get into the office. Trying to enter the combination from inside the office would make too much noise and alert whoever was wandering the bakery to their presence. Feeling her heart pounding in her chest and hoping no one else could hear it, they waited. The footsteps came closer and closer. Someone was just outside the office door. "Dear Lord," Melissa prayed, "make whoever it is go away, please."

The door knob rattled as someone tried turning it but Melissa held it still from her side of the door hoping to give the illusion the door was locked. Then someone began to push on the door. Melissa and Logan held the door in place as best they could. Luckily, the person on the other side wasn't too determined to get into the office. A few moments later, the sound of footsteps on the hard concrete echoed as the person retreated back to the front of the shop. When they heard the front door latch shut, Melissa and Logan began to breathe again and let out simultaneous sighs of relief.

Now that she could breathe again, she was left wishing she had been able to peek out of the office to see who had entered her shop during the waning hours of darkness just before dawn, Melissa silently cursed herself for not at least trying. Maybe it was the killer. She would never know because she had hid in the office. However, she realized she could never have risked Logan's safety by doing so. Reluctantly, she admitted the field trip to the store to investigate had been a bust.

Waiting a while longer, in case the intruder still lurked outside the store, Melissa quickly surveyed her office. Normally the office was neat with everything in its place. That was not the situation now. Her office was a wreck! The small desk had definitely been rifled through. All the drawers were open and papers were flung everywhere. Whether that was the work of the killer, Linda, or the cops, Melissa was afraid she would never know.

The bookcase on the back wall was still standing but all the knick-knacks usually displayed there lay broken on the floor. Even her framed picture of Kevin when he graduated from college with his master's degree in Aviation Science had been knocked over and the glass fractured. Stepping up on her tip toes, Melissa peered at the corner of the bookcase where she had installed a false backing that hid the safe. After close inspection she realized it had indeed been tampered with. The wood was splitting around one side where someone had tried to forcibly remove it. "How could anyone know to look there?" she wondered. Prying the slab away with a letter opener she found on the ground, Melissa was happy to discover that the safe appeared to be intact. The number dial was off though. She always left it on 22; the age she was when she married Kevin. The dial instead showed 18.

Melissa dialed the correct combination to the lock. It popped open. She was shocked to find that the stash of cash she kept on hand was gone. Additionally, her secret recipe box was open with several cards littered about the safe. Looking around the office, she realized there were several recipe cards laying on the ground as well.

Had someone meant to rob her of money and recipes? She could understand someone wanting to swipe her petty cash fund, but the recipe cards? That didn't make sense. Perhaps Linda saw lights on in the shop and came in and disrupted the burglary so the person or persons killed her? Had Linda meant to steal from her? That just seemed odd. What could she have that the "wedding cake wonder" would want? Even so, how would Linda end up dead here? In the Kill Devil Delicacies?

Melissa gathered up the recipe cards as well as the box. Realizing she was removing items from a crime scene, she hesitated before shoving the items into her jacket pocket. As Logan touched his wrist to indicate they were running out of time, she canvassed the office one last time for clues. A few minutes later they were back out the front door and on their way back to her house. The sun would be rising over the Atlantic Ocean in less than a half hour so they quickened their pace. Both were unaware that they were being watched closely. Neither were aware that the traffic camera at the corner of the street had captured their entrance and exit.

## Chapter 5

After sneaking back into her own house to avoid the news crew camped outside, Melissa urged her nephew to get some rest. He lumbered off to his room without complaint. Contemplating her options, she started a pot of coffee brewing and sat down at her kitchen table with the recipe box she had just pilfered from her own shop. She didn't really need the cards anymore. Every recipe was burned into her memory long ago but she liked to keep them around anyway. However, it was odd that some of the cards had been strewn around her office. "Why would anyone want my recipe cards?" she thought.

After 1 ½ large mugs of strong coffee with a splash of French vanilla creamer, the cards were back in their original order. However, a couple were missing. The recipes for her scrumptious Cranberry-Orange bread and her Rosemary Sea Salt bread were not there. Both were big hits with her customers. Melissa even had orders for these breads from tourists that visited their quaint little seaside town during the summer months. The Murphy family was due in town next week and had pre-ordered enough of the Cranberry-Orange bread to feed a small army. The Lucas matriarch from Morgantown, WV paid a year in advance to have the

Rosemary Sea Salt bread delivered every three months to her home. Yes, these two particular artisan breads earned her bakery the most profit, aside from the daily breadsticks and bread bowls for Cheryl's restaurant. She had even planned to enter one of the breads into the first annual Outer Banks Regional Bake-Off to be held next month. The contest boasted that the winner of the artisan bread category would earn a guest spot on a nationally televised cooking show on the Food Network.

Despite not needing the recipes in order to bake any of her breads, Melissa decided to call the police department, at a more reasonable hour, and ask if any recipe cards had been taken into evidence. She couldn't imagine why, but it didn't hurt to ask. Her curiosity was piqued. Mulling over everything that had transpired she wondered:

- Why was Linda in the Kill Devil Delicacies after hours in the first place?
- Was Linda the one that broke in or did she discover the intruder?
- If Linda did break into her shop, why?
- How had someone gotten past her office door security lock, as well as known the location of her safe?

- Who had been in the shop earlier that morning when she and Logan were hiding in the office?

Melissa resolved to find out what information she could from the police but knew she would need to careful. It would not do her any good to let on that she had been in the shop snooping around even with the police tape still cordoning it off. That would certainly add to their suspicions that she was involved in Linda's death. Rubbing her temples to sooth the migraine threatening to come on, she decided that a quick, hot, steamy shower followed by a short nap were in order.

As she was exiting the shower with her hair wrapped up in a plush, pale yellow towel Melissa heard the shrill ring of the house phone. She tripped over a pile of clothes on the floor as she tried to get to the phone. Too late to answer it, the answering machine kicked on just as she made a grab for the handset. The message surprised her immensely. A deep but feminine voice introduces herself as Janice Littleton, an attorney with Dewitt, Pendleton, and Schwartz. The voice continued by stating that she was aware of the "incident" in the bakery and wished to inquire if Mrs. Maples was in need of legal representation. With a slight southern drawl, she ended the message by leaving her contact information.

Melissa was shocked! She had not even considered the possibility that she would need a lawyer. However, following her treatment by the local police yesterday and the obvious interest in her as evidenced by the news van camped outside her home, perhaps obtaining a lawyer was a good idea.

If she wasn't already convinced, the knock on her front door would certainly lead her to that conclusion. Having difficulty getting her clothes on as her body was still damp from the shower, Melissa cursed to herself as she rushed to answer the door. Looking at the clock above the living room fireplace mantle, it was still quite early for visitors. When she opened the door she was greeted by a police badge shoved in her face. Detectives Payne and Reynolds were on her front stoop. The one looking apologetic for disturbing her so early the other looking even grumpier than he had the previous day. The knot in Melissa's stomach became more pronounced as she greeted her guests.

The nicer, and more attractive, gentleman immediately apologized for bothering her so early in the morning, while his partner scowled. Melissa asked what she could do for the officers and if they would like to come in for some coffee. She didn't really want to entertain them but felt kindness would get her more points than outward signs of agitation at their presence. Detective Payne accepted and she moved aside to allow them entry into her home.

Logan had been awakened by the phone ringing and came lumbering out to see who was now at the door. Rubbing his eyes, he was jolted further awake by the sight of the cops in the house. Melissa gave him a reassuring look and encouraged him to get his shower while she spoke with the detectives. She hoped her attempt to appear unflustered by their presence worked. Inside her stomach was in knots and the pain behind her eye increased dramatically.

She offered them coffee and to have a seat at her kitchen table. "Grumpy", as Melissa had decided to refer to him inwardly, took out a notebook and pen as he sat down with the wooden chair creaking underneath his weight. "Mrs. Maples, we have more questions regarding the murder of Mrs. Stevenson in your bakery," he stated while giving her a stern look. "Particularly, we would like to know why you subverted a police barrier this very morning to enter your shop."

Trying to appear nonchalant about the matter, instead of horrified they knew about her visit to the bakery, Melissa smiled as she sat their coffee cups down on the table. Before answering she sat down too. Otherwise, she was afraid her quaking legs would give out from under her. "Detective," she began, "I wasn't trying to 'subvert' anything. I merely needed to retrieve something from my office since it doesn't appear the police are going to allow me to return to my business anytime soon with all the tape around the shop and the place still a mess. I fully intended to call the precinct later to ask a few questions of my own, specifically to see when I can go in to clean up. It really is a disaster in there. There's no way I can re-open anytime soon."

She continued talking, nervous at first but gaining her courage as she went along. "After everything yesterday, no one has told me anything. What happened? How? Why? Does anyone have any idea why Linda was in my bakery in the first place? Do you have any suspects?" Melissa immediately regretted that last question as Grumpy's eyes lit up. Of course they have a suspect – her. Although why they would suspect her, she had no idea.

The nicer one, Detective Payne, kindly answered, "Mrs. Maples, I'm sorry but the investigation is ongoing and we can't release any information. However, we understand your concern since this did happen in your bakery. Of course, you would wish to check out your own shop afterwards to assess the damage and such." With a small grimace he added, "Unfortunately, your place is the scene of a brutal crime that we are still investigating. You cannot cross a police line. By doing so you may have compromised evidence. That, in and of itself, is a crime. We cannot have potential evidence being tampered with, intentionally or unintentionally."

Melissa wondered how she was going to get herself out of this situation. She thought by going there so early that no one would find out. Of course, she hadn't meant to compromise anything. She just needed to see her shop for herself.

Still trying to appear undisturbed, she reassured the officers that she had not meant to jeopardize their investigation at all. Even playing a little dumb, Melissa stated that she hadn't realized that was a possibility and had assumed the police had already obtained all the evidence they needed before they had left the place. She simply needed some of her personal items. If they had explained to her that she could not go back to her own shop before she left the precinct the previous day, Melissa would never have considered it. With a small smile, she looked up hoping to see them convinced she was just ignorant of police procedure and not trying to thwart their investigation. She really wanted them to succeed and find the real killer. However, the skeptical look she was getting from Detective Reynolds clearly said he did not believe her for a second. "This guy really is ready to throw the book at me and he hasn't even tried to find the true culprit," she thought with aggravation.

Luckily, Detective Payne was more receptive of her explanation. He smiled back and calmly told her that they could overlook the trespass this time, since she was not explicitly informed she could not go back to her place of business until the department officially gave the approval. He even added, "We realize all this is upsetting and confusing. We are working relentlessly to determine what happened so justice can be served. Unfortunately, that means your life has be upturned since the crime did happen in your bakery. We are sorry for the disturbance to your business, but in the meantime we ask that you refrain from visiting there." With that last statement, he made to leave.

Melissa found she was sorry to see him go. He was nice and nice looking. Not to mention his voice had a soothing, velvety quality. However, his partner, was quite the other story. He didn't appear nearly satisfied with her response about not knowing she wasn't allowed to cross a police line. Melissa could hardly wait to see the door shut behind him. As they walked out, she decided to push her luck just a little. "Officers," she inquired, "Could you at least tell me if anything was taken from my shop or if you have any idea when I may be allowed back in my shop? The bakery is my livelihood after all and there are bills to pay." The tall, good-looking detective sadly shook his head.

## Chapter 6

Well, if she wasn't sure before she was now. The cops weren't going to be helpful at all. The one had already made up his mind. Even if the surly Detective Reynolds hadn't before, discovering that Melissa had essentially broke into her own bakery…well, that should've cinched it. Muttering under her breath at being so stupid, she didn't hear Logan return to the living room. "That bad, huh?" he finally asked to get her attention. Nodding, she continued to pace the floor.

She kept pondering the same question over and over in her mind. "What should she do now?" The victim was found dead in her bakery. There was known to be animosity between her and the victim. They were considered professional rivals even if they specialized in vastly different areas. She had violated the law by entering her own bakery. She knew money was missing from her safe and a couple recipe cards were now gone but nothing that would add to the death of Linda Stevenson. Of course the cops were going to suspect her. But how could she prove she was innocent and get them to focus on finding the real killer?

Melissa concluded that "The good Lord helps those who help themselves". She had an active interest in finding the real killer. Otherwise, she could end up in jail. She could lose everything. Well, she wasn't going to be able to work for a while. At least not until the cops gave her "permission" to enter her own shop. So, she had the time and the motivation. Melissa was determined to resolve this mystery, with or without help from the actual cops.

While she had been mulling over her options, Logan had fetched the morning paper from the front stoop. Just as he walked back in, a high-pitched female voice broke into Melissa's concentration. "Oh dear!" she fretted, "I forgot all about Britney! The poor girl was probably just as confused as she was, and wouldn't know that she wasn't supposed to go to work."

With her strawberry blonde hair neatly pulled back in a ponytail and dressed for work, Britney waltzed into Melissa's home. The young woman always seemed to be dancing or walking on air. Maybe it was from years practicing ballet or more likely from her recent interest in ball room dancing. Now that Britney was in a serious relationship with the son of one of the wealthiest men on the east coast, she had developed a keen interest in everything the country club set would do. It was starting to annoy Melissa as Britney's practice around the bakery usually led to spilled ingredients all over the floor.

"Hey, boss lady, did you know we're not allowed back in the bakery? Just tried to open up the store and some old geezer with a badge stopped me. Said I was breaking the law or something. Is that crazy or what?" Britney didn't appear too put out that she would be unable to work today. The girl was probably more concerned that she wouldn't be paid.

"Come on in, Brit. Yes, I'm aware. Just had a visit from the same 'old geezer' reminding me to stay away." Melissa offered the young woman some coffee and they sat down to discuss what to do next. Logan, who had a massive crush on Britney, tried acting cool and non-interested in their conversation but Melissa saw him glancing their way a little too often as he ate his bowl of granola on the sofa. It had not escaped his aunt's notice that when Britney came in, he had quickly put the box of sugary kids' cereal back and had taken out the "more adult" granola instead. "Poor kid," she thought, "too young to understand he would never stand a chance with a woman like Britney. Even if he wasn't just a kid, he wasn't from a wealthy family. Rich, trust fund heirs were more her type."

"So now what do we do? Sit around and twiddle our thumbs waiting on the cops?" Britney asked while rolling her eyes to show her personal opinion about the situation. The poor woman had never had a favorable opinion of the police, ever since growing up on the edge of being a juvenile delinquent herself. She had managed to keep her nose clean but had hung out with a bad crowd in high school, including an ex-boyfriend currently doing time up in Raleigh for a robbery spree last year. After growing up poor and taking care of herself since her mom had been too busy boozing it up to be a parent, Britney had recently tasted the good life with her new beau and she wasn't about to mess that up.

Melissa answered carefully, "Actually, I'm not feeling highly confident that the police are going to look further than yours truly for a suspect." She proceeded to fill Britney in on her conversations with the cops and how, at least the one, seemed more than ready to cuff her for the crime and call it a day. Melissa had never been one to just let things happen to her and had already concluded she would have to investigate on her own if she had any hope of remaining free. Inwardly she wanted to rant about the injustice of the whole scenario. How could anyone believe she would do such a thing? Why was she being treated like a suspect rather than a victim since it was her bakery that had been broken into? However, it just wasn't her style. Instead she would rather focus her energies on finding the truth, even if the cops weren't interested in it.

The young woman's blue eyes fairly sparkled with excitement at what her boss intended to do and she wanted in! The two women sat around the table for the rest of the morning concocting a plan. They will need to find out what evidence the police have in custody. Also, someone should speak with Mr. Stevenson to determine why he said all those outrageous lies to the news reporter and see if he knew why his wife was at Melissa's bakery in the first place. Logan tried to appear as if he wasn't listening in but couldn't resist commenting. "Shouldn't we compile a list of possible suspects? Who would have it in for Mrs. Stevenson? Who would also have it in for Aunt Mel?"

"Oh no! There is no way you are involved in this, Logan!" Melissa was not about to allow her beloved nephew to get his hands dirty. Besides her brother would have a heart attack if he found out and his wife would have Melissa's head on a platter if her son got in any sort of trouble. Too bad the boy inherited his stubborn streak from his grandpa, the late Frank Jones and former mayor of Kill Devil Hills. It was the same stubbornness showcased by his Aunt Mel and Uncle Charlie, who was currently serving his fifth tour of duty with the Army in Afghanistan. Whether she wanted his help or not, Logan was in.

# Chapter 7

The trio broke up around noon. The plan was for Britney to visit the Stevenson family to offer her condolences and see what she could discover. Melissa wished she could also go comfort the grieving family but Logan pointed out that it would only cause a scene. Based on Mr. Stevenson's comments the other night, he clearly would not be receptive to a visit from the woman he held responsible.

Melissa would contact the detective with the kind brown eyes on the premise that she was concerned about anything missing from her bakery and was more than willing to cooperate with his investigation. She was a business owner so she had every right to know whatever impacted her business.

Logan, in the meantime, wanted to contact a friend back in Charlotte who was a computer hacking genius. He thought hacking into the police department's server was a good idea to see what the cops had on his aunt. Melissa squashed the idea and forbade him from doing any such thing. However, she remembered that the coroner's son was a big surfer and was often found hanging out at the beach or the Surf Shack, a small surf shop and convenience store. Logan had befriended him a couple summers back so she sent him on an errand to talk to the boy. She doubted he would know anything about his dad's work, but at least the task would keep Logan from breaking the law trying to get into the cop's computers.

As Melissa was heading out the door, a young, twenty-something year old, woman with short blonde hair and dressed in a non-descript grey suit and sensible black pumps, walked up the sidewalk towards her house. At first she thought the woman was a reporter trying to get the scoop from her about Linda's death, but then she recognized the woman from around town. As she approached, the woman smiled and stuck out her hand with a business card. "Hi, Mrs. Maples. I was hoping to find you here. Tried calling you earlier but I am aware you probably are letting all your calls go to voicemail with everything that's going on. Your phone must be ringing off the hook." Looking at the card handed to her, it read "Janice Littleton, Attorney at Law". Deciding she was probably going to need a lawyer sooner or later, Melissa invited the woman inside just as Logan was sneaking out the back in hopes of avoiding the news van parked outside.

Janice quickly introduced herself and explained her reasons for visiting Melissa. There had been a lot of talk around town of the murder of Mrs. Stevenson. Unfortunately for Melissa, a good deal of the talk centered on her being a possible suspect since the two women were known not to be on friendly terms, were even professional rivals, and the fact that the other woman had been found dead in Mrs. Maples bakery. The attorney was quick to point out that she always considered someone innocent until proven guilty. Considering the stuff that was being said about her in connection with the other baker's death, the woman was adamant that Melissa needed a lawyer…immediately.

What could she do but agree? Since she wasn't acquainted with any attorneys and didn't see any others knocking down her door, Melissa hired Janice on the spot. They discussed the case. The lawyer was actually a good source of information as both women jotted down notes as they talked. Apparently, Mr. Stevenson was loudly proclaiming to anyone and everyone that she, Melissa, had it out for his wife ever since she returned to Kill Devil Hills and opened her bakery. This came as somewhat of a shock. She realized Linda hadn't exactly welcomed her back to town but had never held a personal vendetta against the woman. There was no reason for it. Melissa explained her side of the supposed rivalry. She had never considered it a big deal. They knew each other in high school and had a falling out over a guy. Life moved on and so did she. When she came back into town years later and opened the Kill Devil Delicacies,

Melissa didn't even see it as being a competitor with Linda's bakery. Linda did extraordinary wedding cakes. Melissa specialized in breads and dabbled a bit in French pastries. How exactly would that make them true competitors?

Melissa explained to Janice how she and Logan had found Linda's body when they went into work that morning. The back door lock had been busted. She immediately got Logan out of the building and waited for the cops to arrive. End of story. Well, not exactly the end. After being interrogated by the cops for hours and hearing what Mr. Stevenson had to say on the news, she admitted to her newly retained attorney that she had indeed gone back to her bakery just this morning to check on things herself. The young lawyer didn't seem surprised and even said she considered it reasonable that Melissa would do so. Janice agreed with her client that it was strange about the office being broken into, the safe discovered, as well as recipe cards missing. However, she didn't believe missing recipes were vital to the case.

They wrapped up their conversation with more questions remaining than answers. Since she was now officially on the job, Janice mentioned she could start making inquiries at the police station. She also planned to obtain a restraining order against the news crew waiting outside so her client and nephew wouldn't be harassed. Thanking her, Melissa locked the front door as they both headed outside.

## Chapter 8

In the meantime, Britney had gone home to dress in something more suitable to wear to the Stevenson's house. Out of her usual duds and into her nice, new country club attire –pale yellow sundress, white sweater around her shoulders, and white low-heeled sandals. Throwing on her Gucci sunglasses Eddie had given her for their 6 month anniversary, the pretty young woman greeted her boyfriend who had agreed to accompany her on her quest.

Eddie was the quintessential rich boy. Raised by his billionaire shipping magnate father and socialite mother who headed up every charity in town it seemed, Eddie was spoiled. He also suffered from an entitlement complex. Just because of who he was, he believed he should always get what he wanted, when he wanted it. Right now, he wanted two things – promotion at work even though it was really just a job title, he didn't really work; and Britney. The oversized playboy was in love and didn't care that his girlfriend did not hold up to his parents' scrutiny. They recognized a gold digger when they saw one. Actually, his mother had been one herself when she latched onto the senior Mr. Johnson, so she would know.

When they arrived at the Stevenson house, there was hardly any parking available on the street due to the onslaught of locals offering their condolences to the family. Eddie could barely drive his silver Audi R8 Spyder down the crowded street. Grumbling about pebbles chipping the paint job, he helped Britney out of the car. Britney hoped the fact that she worked for Melissa would be overlooked since she was there with Eddie. Otherwise, she doubted anyone would so much as give her the time of day.

The house was overflowing with grieving friends and family. Typical for a small southern town, the kitchen and dining room were overflowing with casserole dishes and vegetable platters. The intent was to provide meals and sustenance for the deceased person's family, but it came off looking like a Pampered Chef party.

The couple mingled with the other mourners. Plenty of the gentlemen there recognized Eddie. Plenty of the women too, but for different reasons. He may be a rich, pompous dude but his beach body, Justin Timberlake good looks still made the ladies swoon. As her beau was overset by men and women alike looking to make his acquaintance or discuss his daddy's business, Britney used the distraction to slink off to other, less occupied parts of the house. Running into the Stevenson's grown daughter Kelly in the hallway, Britney expressed her sympathies to the woman and then feigned she was looking for a bathroom.

With the coast appearing to be clear, Britney tried the door knobs to every room down the corridor. There were just bedrooms and a couple bathrooms until the last door on the left. It was locked. Locked doors didn't faze her. After all, her ex-boyfriend had taught her a valuable skill – picking locks. Pulling a hair pin from her pinned up mane, Britney set to work on the lock. Within seconds she had the door open. "Thank you Carlos," she thought with a smug smile.

The room was an office. By the looks of it – Linda's office. There were pictures and awards displayed all over the walls, including a massive poster of Linda when she was a participant on the reality television series "Amazing Wedding Cakes". On the small oak L-shaped desk were pictures of her children and one of Linda in high school holding a large trophy shaped like a piece of cake. Surprisingly, Britney noticed a young Melissa also in the picture, standing just to the side of Linda with a smaller trophy. Melissa's face had a huge "X" over it in red ink. Deciding that was noteworthy, she took out her brand new iPhone and snapped a picture of the picture.

Britney began to rifle through the contents on top of the desk. There was an application for the Outer Banks Regional Bake-Off that was filled out with a check attached to the form. She didn't consider it unusual for Linda, a baker, to compete in a baking contest so she pushed aside the paper without a second thought. The young woman didn't notice that the entry was for artisan breads, not cakes which were Linda's specialty. If she had, Britney would have been interested to know that Linda had indicated on the application that her entry would be Rosemary Sea Salt bread. This particular bread was a staple of Melissa's baking repertoire.

Not finding anything else in the office worthy of questioning, Britney made to exit the room quickly. With her hand on the door knob, she stopped suddenly at the sound of footsteps coming down the hallway. Waiting, she tried to silently turn the lock in case someone else tried to get into the office and found her there. That would definitely be a bad thing. After a few moments, she heard the bathroom door immediately across the hall open and shut. Britney didn't waste any more time. She vacated the office as quietly and quickly as possible. In her haste, she didn't realize she knocked over the high school picture and some papers had fallen to the floor.

Britney quickly found Eddie deep in conversation with the victim's son about sports cars. Grimacing inwardly, she really hoped he had been more productive in finding out information about the case. Knowing him though, she realized he probably spent the entire time talking about cars and surfing. Good thing she wanted him for his looks and money, not his brain. They continued small talk for a while longer, but Britney was antsy to leave before someone made the connection that she was Melissa's employee. As they made their way out the door, Mr. Stevenson came in from the back yard just in time to see Britney turn to leave. With a sour look on his face, the middle-aged man pulled his phone out of his pants pocket and dialed a number. "Hello, Detective Reynolds please. This is Lloyd Stevenson."

# Chapter 9

"What a glorious day to be at the beach!" Logan raved to himself. The sun was out. A strong breeze was coming off the ocean. The thermometer read 88 degrees. Perfect surfing conditions! Looking out at the waves cresting about 75 yards out, the young man caught sight of his target – the coroner's beach bum son, Tanner – as he strutted back towards The Surf Shack in his wet suit and toting a gleaming smooth surfboard. Yes, Tanner had the life! He didn't have to work in the summers to help save money for college. He spent his days on the beach or on the waves. Not a care in the world.

Logan hailed his friend as he approached the shack. "Dude, you gotta get out there! The sea is ripe today," Tanner stated with somewhat of a slur. Reaching into a small Yeti cooler, the under aged boy pulled out a soda can. At least it looked like a soda can of Mellow Yellow, but under inspection it was easy to spot the flimsy plastic covering a completely different type of beverage. Logan was amazed Tanner could always manage to obtain and keep booze out in the open without being hauled in by the beach patrol. It was a certainty that the boy's father was unaware of his son's habit. At sixteen, the boy was already a lush.

However, this could work to his advantage. Maybe a little tipsy, Tanner would be more likely to open up and inadvertently leak any info he may have overhead from his dad. It was a long shot, since Tanner was as observant as a light pole and had the memory of a blank piece of paper. At this point though, the wayward youth was Logan's best chance to uncover information to help his Aunt Mel.

Tanner offered Logan a can of …well a can of something which he refused. Instead he asked about the waves – a subject Tanner never tired of discussing. It took a while for Logan to transition the conversation to the death of Mrs. Stevenson. Yes, Tanner had heard about the cake lady's demise. No, his father hadn't mentioned anything about the autopsy at home except that it looked like someone bashed in the back of her head with a sharp object. That was the extent of the boy's knowledge of the subject. Logan didn't want the boy reporting back to his dad that the "bread lady's nephew" was asking questions so he didn't push the subject. Based on the stench of his breath, Tanner probably wouldn't even remember the conversation anyway.

As he was about to leave Logan heard a familiar voice from behind him in the shack. It was one of the cops! He turned around to see the incredibly tall younger detective, well younger in relation to his old grump partner. Logan was surprised to see the dude decked out in a wet suit and carrying a board. Somehow it made him look younger. Tanner's expression was priceless. Of course the cop would know his dad. If he smelled his breath or looked too closely at the contents of his cooler, he was in big trouble. The older boy stammered an excuse about being late to meet up with his mom and scurried away.

Detective Payne greeted Logan with a smile as he placed his board down to finish zipping up his suit. "It's Logan, right?" he began. The boy nodded with his eyes wide, wondering if the cop was just being friendly or trying to work an angle to get him to slip up and incriminate himself or his aunt. "It's okay, son. I'm off duty. No interrogations, I promise," he continued. Not knowing whether to believe him or not, Logan shrugged and looked down at his feet.

Trying to break the tension and put the boy at ease the cop took a stab at small talk, "You surf?" Logan nodded again. "There's nothing better than losing yourself in the waves. After everything that's been going on, an hour or so out there will do wonders for one's soul."

"Detective Payne," Logan began but was interrupted.

"Son, the name is Jason out here."

Logan continued, "Ummm, okay. Jason, I'm not sure any amount of surfing would make me feel better right now. I'm not some ignorant little kid. I can tell you guys think my Aunt Mel had something to do with Mrs. Stevenson's death, but I'm telling you the honest to goodness truth – she had nothing to do with it." He wasn't sure what he thought his declaration would accomplish, but couldn't help himself.

Jason responded sincerely, "Logan, I don't personally believe your aunt had anything to do with it. Just following the evidence as any good cop would do. Please trust me, no one in the department is railroading your aunt. I'm sorry for the disruption of your lives while we investigate but there's not a lot I can do to alleviate that at the moment."

"That's not true," the boy said defiantly. "You could at least tell her what's going on. Everyone in town is talking about her. Mr. Stevenson is out there blasting her on the news saying all sorts of lies. And to top it off you guys won't even tell her what happened even though it was her bakery where it all happened. You guys are telling her squat!" He hadn't meant to blurt all that out, but the whole situation was enough to make him pull his hair out. The last couple days were starting to take a toll on him.

Jason calmly put down the surf board. Sitting down on the sun-bleached wooded picnic table he motioned for Logan to join him. "Please, have a seat," he said. He then proceeded to explain to the teenage boy that no one was trying to implicate his aunt. Perhaps his partner had seemed a bit anxious to close the case but that the investigation was nowhere close to being over. He expressed his sorrow that Logan's aunt's name was being dragged through the mud but there was always going to be talk and even the cops couldn't stop people from talking. The officer tried his best to placate the boy's concerns but he could tell Logan was not to be easily swayed so he offered to meet with his aunt to discuss the case, unofficially of course, if he thought that would make her feel better.

Logan considered the detective's offer and decided that he couldn't possibly hurt things at this point. He pulled his phone out of his shorts and speed dialed his aunt. After explaining Jason's offer to her, they agreed that she should meet with him. Since she had been on her way to the precinct to start asking questions there, Melissa altered her route and swung by The Surf Shack.

## Chapter 10

As the sun rose higher in the sky and the temperature rose in unison, Melissa walked up to The Surf Shack where Logan and Jason were quenching their thirst with bottles of orange soda. The boy gave her a Cheshire grin as she approached, knowing he was not allowed soda. It was his aunt's one pet peeve. He was hoping she would overlook the transgression just this once.

While they awaited Melissa's arrival, the two gentlemen had lapsed into a more casual, friendly conversation about surfing and fishing, and even video gaming. Logan was surprised how much the old dude - okay he was only 49 years old but still old in the teenager's eyes – knew about these subjects. He figured the cop was only interested in catching bad guys and donuts. When she found the two together they were laughing as they watched an obvious tourist tween with pasty pale skin trying to boogie board for the first time.

As Melissa walked up to the picnic table, Jason stood up and offered her a seat. Logan noticed a slight glint in the man's eyes and that his aunt blushed ever so softly. "Adults?!" he thought with exasperation.

After exchanging pleasantries, Melissa decided to get to the gist of the matter. She informed Jason that she was keenly aware of the trouble it appeared she was in but she swears she had nothing to do with what happened to Linda. She expressed her sorrow for Linda's death, but she was frustrated with having to stand by while Mr. Stevenson and others were spreading lies that she had any reason to want to hurt Linda because she absolutely didn't. While the other woman's body had been discovered in her bakery, she asserted that she was the one that called the cops in the first place and had since been treated as a suspect instead of an additional victim. Her business was broken into. A grisly murder had happened in there. She wasn't even allowed back in to assess the damages or determine if something was missing. Frustrated, she asked, "How exactly am I supposed to clear my name and get my life back if no one at the police department will even tell me what's going on?"

Jason listened intently to the captivating baker for quite a while before attempting to reply. He kept having to remind himself to stop staring into her large, almond-shaped hazel eyes and to keep his brain from fixating on how the gold flecks in her eyes flashed as she passionately stated her case. He had to physically shake his head to re-focus on what she was saying.

Still, her words sunk in and he was compassionate to her plight, but he couldn't allow compassion to blind him to the evidence that was currently sitting in clear plastic bags in the department's evidence room. He didn't believe it was fair that she was completely unaware of just how much all the clues were pointing to her.

Melissa continued, "I realize that the case is ongoing and all that gibberish, but this is my life on the line here. My good name. While that may not mean much to anyone else in this town, it's all I have left." Without realizing what he was doing, Jason reached across the table and took her hands in his own.

While Jason couldn't reveal specifics he was able to fill her in on a few facts as it related to her bakery. Forensics had taken a number of fingerprints. Most of the prints had been ruled as belonging to her, Britney, and Linda. There was one other partial print that they had not been able to identify. It was being sent off to the local FBI office for further analysis. Additionally, the back door had been broken into but it didn't appear the intruder knew a lot about breaking locks. Most likely the intruder was an amateur and the police had not ruled out that Linda had been the one breaking into the bakery. The question on everyone's minds was "Why?"

Melissa asked about her office. Since he was already aware she had visited the scene, she didn't think it would hurt to broach the subject. Jason told her that they had noticed the door to the office was unlocked and had taken evidence from the room, but that only a couple recipe cards had been located in Mrs. Stevenson's fanny pack which she was wearing at the time she was found dead. They had not been aware any cash was missing. Melissa explained that she usually kept $1,200 petty cash on hand which should have been in the safe. Jason agreed to add that to the case file but he doubted they would find such a small sum of cash.

By the end of their conversation, Jason and Melissa agreed that they should go back to the bakery together, in an official capacity so he could log a list of missing items. That way she could also see the place in broad daylight and pick up any items she might need between now and whenever the police department gave the go ahead to re-open the shop. When asked for a guesstimate for when that may be, Jason only shrugged his shoulders. He decided to forego his surfing expedition for the day and instead would change back into his street clothes so they could head over to the Kill Devil Delicacies bakery.

# Chapter 11

Despite it being mid-afternoon on a hot summer day, Melissa felt chilled as they entered the bakery. Unlocking the front door, she felt more than saw the multitude of eyes staring at her from along the street. Logan, being less intimidated, turned around and stared at all the gawkers causing them to quickly turn back around and get back to their own businesses.

Flicking on the lights, nothing seemed out of place in the front of the bakery. There was still powder residue on the counter and cash register from where the police took fingerprints. The real story was in the back. Jason asked them not to touch anything. If they needed to check anything or pick something up, he would do so with latex gloves so as not to contaminate the scene. Melissa gave him the code to open the cash register. Nothing in there but she informed him that Britney had taken the cash, all except what was kept in the safe, to the bank depository the night in question. Finding nothing out of the ordinary in the front, the trio approached the door to the back room with hesitation. To be honest, Melissa was not looking forward to seeing dried blood all over her floors. It brought fresh images to her mind of finding Linda's body.

The back room was much like Melissa remembered from the other night. Jason asked if she noticed anything out of place. Well, of course she did! Everything seemed out of place! Utensils and bread pans littered the counters and the floor. She was a neat freak when it came to her cooking area so the scene before her was a nightmare. He informed her that most of the items that may have contained a trace of blood or a fingerprint had been confiscated and were now in the evidence room at police headquarters. Looking around at the mess that used to be her sanctuary, Melissa felt nauseous.

Finally, they walked over to the office. Melissa indicated where the safe was located. Opening the safe, she restated that she always kept $1,200 in the safe as a petty cash fund or for emergencies. Clearly, there was no money in there now. Reluctantly, she also told him about the recipe box, explaining that she had taken the box and what cards she found home under the guise that she may need the recipes in order to bake at home if she wasn't allowed back in her own shop. After sorting the cards at home, she discovered two were missing from her stack – Rosemary Sea Salt and Cranberry-Orange breads. Jason agreed to check the evidence log to see if these were the particular cards that had been found on the deceased woman's person. He also chastised her for removing potential evidence from the scene even if he did agree they probably weren't important to the case.

He felt the missing money was more of a legit reason for the break-in. But that raised another question – Who besides Melissa knew about the cash and the location of the safe? Britney knew where the safe was but did not know the combination. Anyway, if Britney was interested in money, she had access to a lot more cash than $1,200 since she deposited over $5,000 that night at the bank. If she needed money, she could easily have taken that. Besides, the young woman also had an extremely wealthy boyfriend to take care of all her monetary needs.

There was still the biggest question of them all – Why had Linda Stevenson been inside the Kill Devil Delicacies bakery at all?

They didn't have time to mull the question over as Jason's phone unexpectedly rang, startling all three. Melissa and Logan had a good laugh as they were surprised to discover Jason's ring tone wasn't the normal tones found on any cellular phone. No, his was "Kick Start My Heart" by Motley Crue which didn't seem to fit his clean-cut cop persona. Jason answered the phone and carried on a short conversation. Afterwards, he gave Melissa a worried look. "Sorry to have to cut this short," he explained, "I'm needed back at the precinct. Seems your assistant has been brought in for questioning. Apparently, Mr. Stevenson suspects she was snooping around his house today."

## Chapter 12

"Miss Williams, please just answer the question," Detective Reynolds implored. The poor man was quickly running out of patience with the young woman. "Attractive or not," he thought, "she's a real piece of work." After receiving the call from Mr. Stevenson, he had immediately sent a couple of rookies over to Britney's house to bring her in for questioning and another cop of two years over to the Stevenson house to get a statement from Mr. Stevenson and any other visitors that witnessed Britney's irregular visit to the home. Lloyd Stevenson was raging mad and throwing around all sorts of accusations that the woman was there for some nefarious purpose and probably sent there by her boss. Personally, Detective Reynolds was glad he able to stay here instead of dealing with the grieving man. Lloyd wasn't someone you wanted to deal with on a regular basis, even if in a happy occasion. The death of his wife would make the usual hostile man only worse.

Unfortunately, the woman wasn't proving very helpful. She wouldn't say a word except "I will not say anything without my lawyer present." He figured she probably learned that from watching some silly cop show on television. Anyway, he was forced to wait for her attorney who was in no hurry to arrive apparently. When Peter Andrews, a Johnson Family's lawyer, finally did arrive the detective was more annoyed. Of course, Edward Johnson Jr. would send one of his dad's fleet of attorneys to protect his little precious snowflake from the big bad cops. Sitting across from Miss Williams and the oversized buffoon that was this hot-to-trot lawyer in the cramped interview room, Larry rubbed the bridge of his nose to ward off a headache. "I'm too old for this," he mused to himself.

Every question he asked, she looked over at Mr. Andrews, the lawyer, who would nod or shake his head for her to answer. The entire process took over three hours and he didn't glean much information from it. Yes, she was a bakery assistant at the Kill Devil Delicacies owned by Mrs. Melissa Maples. Yes, she had been at the Stevenson house with her boyfriend offering their condolences to the family. Yes, she had encountered the Stevenson daughter as she searched for a bathroom. No, she had not spoken with Mr. Stevenson as she did not see him when she was there. They left the house within 45 minutes to an hour after arriving.

Not a lot to go on for the tired detective. Larry had to hope the cop at the Stevenson home found some evidence of something or this was just another dead end. He was just wrapping up the interview when his partner finally decided to show up. As he walked the attorney and young woman out, he noticed the younger Mr. Johnson waiting anxiously. As if on cue, Andrew's voice raised a couple octaves as he chastised the police for wasting his client's time. Larry almost laughed since it was obvious the lawyer was putting on a show for the benefit of the lazy, entitled Mr. Johnson Jr. but thought better of it since being sued right before retiring was not on his personal bucket list.

Jason also thought it was a bit of overkill since the woman had not been harassed at all, just questioned in an ongoing case. It certainly made sense to interview her. She was an employee of Melissa's and had access to the bakery. The attorney was making an ordinary police procedure into a bigger case than it was. Britney wasted no time in running over to her beau as if she had just undergone the inquisition. With a stern look to the detectives and a friendly handshake with the designer suit attorney, Eddie escorted the fair "damsel in distress" out of the precinct and sped away in his prized Audi.

Before following his client out the door, the Mr. Andrews turned around with a final warning that he would be on the lookout for any ill treatment or harassment of Miss Williams and her boss in the future and the police department had better take more care. Stunned, the detectives both processed this final statement differently. Jason questioned why Eddie Johnson Jr. and Britney were so jumpy. What did they have to fear? Larry's mind latched onto the part that mentioned Britney's boss as well. The interview had been about Britney and her visit to the Stevenson's house. He had never mentioned her boss, Mrs. Maples, so why did the big shot lawyer?

## Chapter 13

In the meantime, Melissa and Logan were arriving home after their visit to the bakery. The news van was still parked around the corner. Before she had a chance to react, a young twenty-something female in a smart suit and holding a microphone ran up to them followed by a heavy set man carrying a large camera. Melissa tried to get the front door open but dropped the keys in her haste. Desperate to get Logan away from the prying eyes of the news, she didn't even hear the barrage of questions flying out of the reporter's mouth. To Melissa, she sounded like the teacher from the old Peanuts cartoons. However, she did hear Logan loud and clear, "No comment! Leave my aunt alone!"

They were miraculously saved when a booming voice from the direction of the sidewalk ordered the news people to leave now before he called the cops and had them arrested for harassment. Melissa had never been so glad to see Luis in all her life. Luis was a giant of a man at 6'4" with the body of an aging WWE wrestler. He also owned the only other bakery in town, next to Melissa's and Linda's. He specialized in traditional bakery fare – cakes, cupcakes, pies, and the best marzipan to be found on the east coast. Melissa was also good friends with his wife, Maria. At least once a month the two women, usually joined by Cheryl, would have a ladies' night out.   Also, the two women were old friends from high school. Maria had been thrilled when Melissa moved back to town.

As Luis used his hulking frame to shield them from the reporters, Melissa snatched her keys off the ground and the group bolted through the front door, slamming it on the nosy cameraman who was still trying to get video footage. Luis issued a string of curse words but then looked apologetically over at Logan. The look on the young boy's face was priceless. His aunt was a bit worried there were much worse words floating around in his head than what came out of Luis's mouth. In the melee, she hadn't even noticed that Maria was with her husband.  Now safely inside she gave them both a hug of thanks.

"Luis, you are an angel!" she proclaimed. The big man just shrugged off the praise. Maria, on the other hand, began fussing over Melissa and Logan. She was always the mother hen type. Before she knew it, Maria had taken over her kitchen and was fixing them all some tea and sandwiches. Melissa, for perhaps the first time since this ordeal began, relaxed on her comfy, oversized sofa.

With everyone taken care of, Maria sat down with the group in the living room. They discussed what had happened to Linda, of course. Melissa filled them in on the events from her vantage point with Logan interjecting with a few quips here and there, mostly about the incredibility that that anyone would believe Aunt Mel had something to do with the situation. His aunt smiled fondly at the boy. He was being very overprotective. She just hoped he didn't take it too far. He was sometimes a hot-headed teenager after all.

Maria and Luis expressed their confidence that the cops would come to their senses and wrap the case up soon, exonerating Melissa in the process. However, they had come over to warn her about the trouble Mr. Stevenson was causing. He had spoken to nearly a dozen news stations in North Carolina and even one national news outlet. What he had to say about Melissa was beyond slander. He outright accused her of being the one to kill his wife because she (Melissa) "despised and hated Linda all her life and had purposefully come back to Kill Devil Hills to ruin his wife's business." The whole idea was preposterous! Melissa couldn't comprehend how anyone would think that of her. So they didn't get along after high school? So they weren't big buddies when she moved back to town? How does that add to wanting to kill someone? The four agreed it was bizarre. Perhaps the man was so grieved by her death he was lashing out at the first person he could think of, which would be Melissa since Linda was found in her bakery.

Looking up, Melissa noticed a strange expression on Maria's face. She knew something else but was hesitant to say it. Taking the hint, she instructed Logan to freshen up with a nice long shower since it had been such a long day already, and it wasn't over yet. At first the boy resisted but seeing the purposeful look on his aunt's face, he decided to make himself scarce for a little while.

"Okay, there's something you are not telling me, Maria. What is it?" What she heard sounded even crazier than the idea that she had something to do with Linda's death. Yes, it was true that Linda had never welcomed Melissa back to town with open arms and she was aware that the woman gossiped about her behind her back. She had heard a few of the stories – Melissa supposedly envied Linda since high school and had always tried copying her and being better than her at everything and since moving back to town she was still doing it. Well, that was nuts! Melissa never wasted her time on envy or thinking twice about Linda after their falling out in high school. Apparently, that was not the case for Linda. There had also been a rumor started, she assumed by Linda, that Melissa was too selfish of a person to even have children and that was why she remained childless. This had really infuriated Melissa when she heard that one after being back in town for a few months. Melissa and Kevin had desperately wanted children and had spent most of their life earnings and savings trying to get pregnant to no avail. Yet had it angered her enough to want Linda dead? No. Absolutely not.

Maria then asked Melissa if she had entered the Outer Banks Regional Bake-Off. She had, of course. It was quite an opportunity since the winner would be a guest on a nationally televised cooking show. As soon as she heard about the contest, she had sent in her entry form. Her friend informed her that Linda also planned to enter the contest. It wasn't unusual since Linda always did like the spot light and had even been on a televised cooking contest a few years back. However, it was strange given that this particular contest was targeted toward artisan breads, not wedding cakes which were Linda's specialty. Although a wizard with cakes, Linda didn't even offer breads in her bakery. For her to enter a contest for artisan breads did seem a bit odd. Luis added that while at the grocery store a couple weeks back he had overheard Linda say she intended to beat Melissa at her own game. From the sound of the conversation, it sounded like her primary goal was simply to humiliate her rival. Melissa couldn't understand Linda's continued outright hatred of her all these years. Sadly, she wondered if perhaps there was a little something "off" about the woman. Did mentally healthy people hold on so tightly and so bitterly to what to most would be considered minor grudges?

This information got Melissa to thinking. Could the bake-off be related to why Linda was in her bakery when she was killed? Could this be tied to the missing recipe cards? Both breads were known to be Melissa's very best and she had intended on entering one into the contest. It seemed so silly that this whole fiasco was over a baking contest, but she couldn't rule anything out.

"There's something else you should know," Luis began. "We don't know this for a fact. It's more gossip at this point, but there has been some talk that Linda and Lloyd were having marital problems." Melissa was stunned. The couple always appeared to be the epitome of the happy-ever-after husband and wife. They were never seen in public when they weren't holding hands. Besides, Linda would tell anybody and everybody that would listen just how happy they were together and how blessed she felt. How Linda's marriage fit into this story was unclear but again, it was something to go on.

Logan came back into the room as the trio were speculating if and how this information played into the other woman's demise and the break-in at the Kill Devil Delicacies. Melissa vowed to call Jason the next morning about the information, but neither Luis nor Maria thought it was a good idea. Well, if not the detective, she decided she should at least let her newly hired lawyer know. The adults turned the conversation to more amiable subjects for the boy's benefit. He never let on that he had overheard everything. It was enough to whet his curiosity and he fully intended to find out more.

Later that evening, Melissa made the mistake of turning on the television after the group had enjoyed a wonderful, authentic Spanish meal compliments of Maria. There on her 32 inch Sony flat screen was video of Lloyd Stevenson holding a press conference in front of his home. He was railing against the police department for dragging their feet and not arresting someone for the brutal murder of his sweet wife. According to him, everyone knew who was guilty of the crime and there was no excuse for why that woman was not behind bars that very second. He went on to detail how the "guilty party" had even gone so far as to send in her employee to snoop in his own home as his family grieved. In the background, his adult children were clearly visible with his daughter sobbing and his son standing stoically holding her hand.

Before they had a chance to watch the entire scene play out, Luis grabbed the remote and turned the TV off. Melissa was shocked into silence. Not the case for Logan. The boy was beyond angry at this point.

"How dare that man attack my aunt?!" He ranted and raved for several minutes before collapsing on the sofa next to Melissa, near tears. Dumbfounded, she took his hands in her own. Without words, the two consoled each other. Luis and his wife stayed a couple more hours to care for their friend and her distraught nephew. Neither believed Melissa was guilty of doing any harm to Linda. Neither could understand Lloyd Stevenson's public display of outrage, even for a supposed grief-stricken man. The situation was spiraling out of control fast. They just hoped somewhere along the line common sense would prevail before their friend ended up in jail for a crime she could not possibly have committed.

## Chapter 14

Melissa received a call from Britney late in the evening informing her that the young woman had been brought in for questioning by the police. This on top of everything else contributed to a fitful night's sleep. Not rested at all, Melissa woke up even earlier than usual. She could hear Logan's gentle snores coming from his room. What she really wanted to do was go for a long walk to clear her head, but with the high probability of being harassed by reporters, she settled for a large cup of coffee and some leftover marzipan to be enjoyed on her deck. It was still pitch black dark and a bit chilly so she wrapped up in her fuzzy robe.

She replayed all the events of the last couple days over and over again in her mind, trying to make sense of everything. What she knew was:

- Linda was found dead in her bakery.
- Someone had broken into her bakery through the back door. Was it Linda or someone else?
- The cash from the safe was missing as well as two particular recipe cards - Rosemary Sea Salt bread and Orange-Cranberry bread.

- Linda had intended to enter the Outer Banks Regional Bake-Off artisan bread contest.
- It seemed Linda's primary goal had been simply to defeat Melissa in the contest out of leftover spite from high school.
- Linda had a picture on her home office desk from high school with Melissa's face crossed through. Disturbing.
- Lloyd Stevenson was telling anyone and everyone that Melissa was guilty, although she was unaware of any evidence against her.
- It was rumored that Lloyd and Linda were having marital issues.

Nothing added up. There had to be something she was missing.

Just as the sun started to rise, Melissa's phone rang. First it was her brother checking on Logan. He was running late to the airport for a business trip to Chicago so it was a brief chat. She really thought he would be more concerned about his son being in the midst of all this chaos.

Shortly after another call came in from her newly hired attorney, Janice. Apparently, she had been burning the midnight oil as she had more information about the case. She confirmed that Lloyd and Linda Stevenson were having problems with their marriage.

The now deceased wife had hired a private detective several months ago to keep track of her husband's whereabouts. The detective had handed over his files to the police already but kept copies for himself. Just a couple weeks ago he had presented Linda with the evidence against her husband which showed he frequented a strip club, and suspected brothel, in Nags Head. There were pictures of him coming out of the club with a bleach blonde, leggy woman.

Janice went on to add that Linda had requested the detective check into Lloyd's finances. He had uncovered that her husband had taken out a substantial life insurance policy on Linda about one year ago. $1.5 million to be exact. She had not known about the policy until that time. When she found that out, the detective said Linda had raged that she wouldn't allow him to get away with this. He assumed she meant that she would file for divorce but he never heard back from her.

All this was highly interesting information. Perhaps Lloyd killed his wife or had someone do it for him but he had to place blame elsewhere. The known dislike Linda and Melissa felt for each other was enough to make the accusation look legitimate while keeping the focus off of himself. Janice was confident that if the private investigator's files were already in police custody, they could put two and two together. Sadly, Melissa was not so certain.

She was right to doubt. A couple hours after the call with her lawyer ended, there was a knock at the front door. Melissa opened the door to find Detectives Payne and Reynolds, along with an entire team of uniformed cops. Detective Reynolds shoved a piece of paper in her face as Jason apologized for the intrusion but there had been a tip called into the precinct the night before. The paper was a search warrant for her home and for her bakery.

## Chapter 15

By the time the police finished with searching her home, Melissa felt violated. Nothing had gone untouched. Her computer was taken into custody for something Jason called "forensic review". Her clothes were dumped onto her bed as they rummaged through her dresser and closet. Same with Logan's things. The kitchen was a disaster zone with utensils and cooking equipment strewn along the countertops and table. When she thought there couldn't possibly be anywhere else for them to look, a couple officers headed outside to the garbage bins behind the house. Melissa watched with dismay as they turned over the bins allowing the contents to fall onto the small lawn. She certainly hoped they planned to clean all this up, but she wasn't very optimistic.

During the search, she and Logan had been instructed to wait outside. They retreated to the back deck area so they could still see what was happening inside the house through the French doors. Detective Payne played things strictly by the book. However, he gave her a few apologetic looks, especially when he noticed an officer mishandling her things or in general making a huge mess. A couple times a uniformed officer placed something in a plastic bag

and handed it off to another for safe keeping. Melissa
assumed these items were being taken as evidence,
but had no idea why. The recipe box was one of these
items. Other baking items were also included –
serrated bread and cake knives, a stainless steel
curved kiss knife, a dough cutter/scraper, cheese
knife, and a pear corer. It appeared the search was for
sharp baking instruments. Then an officer came out of
her laundry room with all the dirty clothes from the
last few days. Wryly, Melissa hoped they intended to
take the clothes to be washed, dried, and folded. The
one household task she liked the absolute least was
laundry. Every time someone bagged an item,
Detective Reynolds would write something down on
his notepad and cast a suspicious look her way.
Melissa's patience with that man was about to reach
its breaking point.

Initially, Logan very loudly objected to what the cops
were doing to his aunt's house. She managed to calm
him down. Melissa wasn't happy about the situation
either, but was smart enough to realize that arguing
would only make matters worse at this point. As her
house was being destroyed and her things taken as
evidence, she could only look on in horror at the mess
her life had become in such a short time.

Jason informed them that a similar search was being
conducted at the bakery. Melissa didn't understand
why they had to search there again. Hadn't they

already discovered whatever there was to discover there when Linda was first found? He shook his head "no". He quietly explained that a tip had been called in giving very specific information about items that may or may not be in Melissa's home and at the bakery. Part of his job was to follow up on every lead. Considering she knew she wasn't guilty of anything, Melissa suspected that the "tip" had been called in by Linda's husband. He seemed to enjoy causing trouble for her. When she asked Jason, he gave the expected response, "We can't discuss any details of the case at this time."

"Now that's total bull and you know it! You're invading my home and treating me and my nephew like criminals. I have a right to know what is going on!" she angrily retorted. Melissa was normally a very mild-tempered person. It took a lot to push her buttons. This really had gone too far. Feeling her blood boil, she didn't want to make a scene in front of Logan. The boy had really gone through too much for such a young man. It wouldn't be fair to him if she lost her cool now. She tried to calm herself so he wouldn't hear the tremble in her voice. Realizing she wasn't going to get any information from Jason, she continued to sit on her deck and watch as the police turned her house upside down looking for something that couldn't possibly be found – evidence – because she wasn't guilty!

As the police wrapped up their search of her home, Jason's phone rang. She only heard one side of the conversation, but it didn't bode well as far as she could tell. The normally calm cop became quite agitated. He brusquely barked orders to whoever was on the other end of the line to "bag everything" and to leave a patrol at the front and back of the bakery.

With the call ended, he motioned for Detective Reynolds to join him in the kitchen. The only highlight of this entire ordeal occurred as the stouter, shorter officer tripped over some baking pans littering the tiled kitchen floor. Both Melissa and Logan giggled loudly. Even a few of the uniformed cops that remained inside the house found it difficult to suppress a chuckle or smile. As the older gentleman flashed angry glances around the room, his eyes landed on Melissa. The look on his face was easy to read. He was ticked off. For whatever reason he had it in for her. All he had to do was wait for the right piece of evidence so he could lock her up. His malicious stare assured her that he already believed her guilty and would stop at nothing to prove it. She just hoped he wasn't in such a rush to convict her that he overlooked evidence that would exonerate her.

That hope was dashed as the two detectives ended their confab in the kitchen. With a sad look on Jason's face and a gleam of satisfaction from the other detective, they walked out to the deck. "Mrs.

Melissa Maples, you are under arrest for the murder of Linda Stevenson. You have the right to remain silent. Anything you say can and will be used against you in a court of law. You have the right to talk to a lawyer and have him/her present while you are being questioned. If you cannot afford to hire a lawyer, one will be appointed to represent you before any questioning if you wish. You can decide at any time to exercise these rights and not answer any questions or make any statements," Detective Reynolds said with a smile. He continued, "Mrs. Maples, do you understand each of these rights as I have explained them to you?" Stunned speechless, Melissa responded the only way she could by a slight nod of her head.

## Chapter 16

It was Melissa's first time in the back of a police squad car. She dearly hoped it would be her last. Jason kindly volunteered to stay behind with the distraught teenager until friends arrived to care for the boy. Before he handcuffed her, he offered to call Maria and Luis for her. He also tried to reassure her that Logan would be okay. Melissa highly doubted that since the poor boy had just watched his beloved aunt be arrested. She instructed Logan to call his parents to let them know what was going on. Detective Reynolds overheard and gruffly stated that Logan wouldn't be going anywhere as he was designated as a potential witness. He even had the audacity to suggest that Logan could be upgraded to a potential accomplice to murder. "Now that really is bull----!" she retorted.

At least the ride to the precinct was short. The elderly detective used the time to completely infuriate Melissa as he hummed happily the entire trip. Melissa thought of more than a few words to call the man. None of those words were polite. After being booked - complete with a not-so-lovely mug shot, the confiscation of all her belongings, and being fingerprinted - the detective led Melissa to a small interrogation room where he handcuffed her to the table. "This may be a good time to allow me a phone call to my attorney," she tersely requested. Nodding, he brought over a cordless phone and left the room.

Needless to say Janice Littleton was shocked when she received the call. She had not expected her client to be arrested for the crime. Suspected? Yes, but clearly there was insufficient evidence. Within less than a half hour, she burst through the precinct door demanding to see her client. Detective Reynolds directed her to the interrogation room. He already turned on the recording device in the tiny room behind the two-way mirror.

Janice greeted a weary and distraught Melissa with a warm hug. She asked about Logan and if he was being cared for by friends or family. Once assured the boy was in good hands, the attorney informed her client that her assistant was already working on the bail hearing. Based on Melissa's outstanding reputation in the community, she felt they had an excellent chance of getting her released on her own recognizance.

Melissa explained that she had no idea what prompted her arrest. The police showed up at her home, and at the bakery, with search warrants. They trashed her house. She suspected they trashed her business, too. However, no one had seen fit to tell her what implicated her to such an extent that she was now in handcuffs.

As if on cue, Detective Reynolds and Detective Payne entered the room. Based on the size of the area, it was quickly getting crowded in there. Janice ordered them to explain what charges were being filed against her client and the basis for their accusation. Otherwise, she instructed them to release her client immediately. The older gentlemen chuckled, "Oh, we have plenty to base our conclusions on." Jason didn't look so convinced. That wasn't much, but it was something for Melissa to hold onto to in order to retain her sanity.

Both women sensed Detective Reynolds would not be any help whatsoever. Melissa took a chance. "Detective Reynolds, why don't you do us all a favor and go back to your little observation room," as she nodded toward the two-way mirror, "and…observe." Continuing, she said, "Detective Payne is more than capable of asking questions and answering our questions without your…help."

His reaction was priceless. Melissa swore his face and neck turned the color of a pomegranate in less than two seconds. Even Jason and Janice couldn't help but smile at her gumption. Jason attempted to calm his partner by assuring him that he had everything under control. It didn't do much good. The older gentlemen was livid. After storming out of the room, Melissa couldn't control it any longer. She laughed, even though she knew the detective could still hear her.

"Oh dear, I'm so sorry but I just can't take that man anymore," she apologized. Jason reassured her that he completely understood. However, he also warned it was not a good idea to tick off his partner. The man knew how to hold a grudge. Melissa responded, "For some reason, I think he already harbors a grudge against me or has it out for me. For the life of me, I don't understand why. Throughout this entire ordeal, he's been a complete…" she struggled with the right word as the real one in her mind would really not help matters, "…jerk."

With the tension somewhat subdued, Jason informed Melissa of the entire list of charges against her. So far there was one charge for second degree murder – murder without premeditation. Then there was a charge of evidence tampering. Another charge for interfering, hindering, or opposing a police officer by crossing a police line.

"Well, I can tell you that I absolutely, positively did NOT murder anyone!" Melissa affirmed. "However, we both know I went back to the bakery and crossed the yellow line, but honestly I did not know it was against the law to go into my own business." At this point, Janice attempted to "shush" her and advised that she not say anymore. She also shot an annoyed look to the two-way mirror and directed her next statement to it. "Why don't you do something useful and get my client's bail hearing scheduled?"

The attorney questioned what evidence the police had and how had they obtained a search warrant. Jason admitted he was not present when the warrants were obtained. His partner had them ready to go when he came into work that morning. The only thing Reynolds said was that an anonymous tip had been called in. Janice questioned how the police determined the tip had been from a credible source. Again, Jason shrugged to indicate he was not aware of the answer. "You didn't think to question your partner before heading over to my client's house and place of business?" the lawyer asked sternly.

The detective only responded that he trusted his partner. Neither Melissa nor Janice were convinced the older detective was trustworthy. The expressions on their faces were all too readable what they thought of Detective Reynolds.

Jason attempted to move the discussion away from his partner. He continued to explain the evidence that had led up to Melissa's arrest. Several items were taken into custody at the time the police were initially called to the scene – baking utensils, some knives, etc. However, testing revealed that none of these were the murder weapon. Also, fingerprints lined up as expected to belong to Melissa, Britney, and Logan as they worked there. Initially, there just wasn't a lot to go on except the crime occurred in the Kill Devil Delicacies. This alone made Melissa a suspect.

"Officer, none of this is enough to warrant arresting my client," Janice warned. He nodded in agreement and continued. There were a couple other partial prints which were determined to belong to Mrs. Stevenson and Edward Johnson, Jr. Melissa explained that Eddie sometimes picked Britney up from work so it would not be unusual to find his prints. However, she still didn't understand why Linda was there in the first place.

The detective enlightened them a bit on that topic. Apparently, Mr. Stevenson informed the police, and anyone that would listen, that Melissa had called his wife earlier that day and asked her to stop by the bakery later in the evening. He thought it was odd since the two women notoriously did not get along. Jason asked, "Did you contact Mrs. Stevenson at any time and request she visit you at your shop?"

"Of course not," an angry Melissa retorted. "You have my phone in custody. Check the flipping call log!" In her mind, they simply co-existed in the same town. There weren't friends, but she didn't consider Linda an enemy either. However, as of late, it seemed

Linda had thought differently. Jason nodded as he jotted down her answers on a flimsy notebook pad.

He repeated a lot of the questions that had been asked the first time the police took her statement. Where was she on the evening in question? What time did she leave the bakery? Was she the one to lock-up? And so on and so forth. The line of questioning really frustrated her. The questions had already been answered. Still, a reason for the search warrants and her arrest had not been provided.

According to Jason, Mr. Stevenson had become suspicious after seeing Britney at his house. When questioned, she claimed she was simply there to offer her condolences along with her boyfriend. However, she never even approached Mr. Stevenson, the grieving husband. The cops were called out to take another statement from Mr. Stevenson when he called the police to inform them of the young woman's presence at his house. They discovered that someone had been in Linda's home office at some point during the day. He claimed that the office had been locked since the morning before his wife's murder. Mr. Stevenson suspected, and outright accused, Britney of snooping at his home. He also asserted she probably did so under orders from her boss.

Then the detective dropped a bombshell on them. During the search of the bakery, a sharp item was found wedged in between the office desk and the wall. It was a large, stainless steel serrated cheese knife covered in the victim's blood. Shock was apparent on Melissa's face. Being a cop for a long time, Jason felt confident in his people-reading skills. Her expression was one of genuine surprise and horror. Personally convinced she was not guilty, he wasn't allowed to let his intuition overrule the facts of the case.

Reluctantly, he said, "There's more." Jason told them the missing $1,200 cash was found stuffed into a laundry detergent container in her recycling bin.

When questioned, Melissa vehemently denied knowing how the money got there. She also knew nothing about the knife. Yes, she probably owned several knives just like the one described. Still…she didn't kill Linda! "What possible motive would I have had to kill her?" she asked.

At that, Detective Reynolds re-emerged from behind the looking glass. "Mrs. Maples, it is well known that the two of you had a distinct dislike for each other going back as far as high school. Additionally, you were business rivals." Melissa started to object by saying that not being fond of someone for years was no reason to kill them. Also, she didn't consider them to be business rivals. They specialized in two distinct baking areas that did not intersect. Surely there was plenty of room in the small seaside town for them both to have been successful. The look on his face said he wasn't convinced.

"Mrs. Maples, isn't it true that you entered the Outer Banks Regional Bake-Off?" She nodded. "And what exactly were you planning to bake for the contest?" Melissa recalled considering her two best-known breads - Cranberry Orange bread and Rosemary Sea Salt bread. She eventually decided on the Rosemary Sea Salt recipe. The older detective continued, "Were you aware that Mrs. Stevenson also intended to compete in the Bake-Off?" Before she had a chance to answer, he moved on to his next question. "Were you also aware that Mrs. Stevenson planned to enter the contest with her own Rosemary Sea Salt bread?"

## Chapter 17

Hours later, Detective Payne emerged from the police station exhausted. He and his partner had questioned Melissa for a large portion of the day. The rest had been spent reviewing all the evidence obtained from her home and business. Just a couple hours ago, the call came in that a bail hearing was set for 9:00 a.m. tomorrow. He hated that the pretty baker had to spend even one night behind bars. Truly, he believed she was innocent. However, he had not yet determined any other suspects for the murder nor who set Melissa up to take the fall.

Jason drove away from the station in his beat-up red Chevy truck. His mind swirled with countless questions. Nothing about this case made sense to him. Murder over artisan bread? Really? There had been a lot of nutty cases in Kill Devil Hills throughout the years. This one took the proverbial cake.

He decided against going straight home. No one waited for him there anyway. Not since his ex-wife Chrissy left him for some Army ranger-type living in Elizabeth City. He didn't mind the loss of his wife. The few years of wedded bliss had been anything but blissful. His only regret was he missed out on the everyday life of his daughter. Madeline was now a junior in high school. She visited occasionally, but never long enough or often enough for her dad's wishes.

Before Jason realized it, he drove past a large local church where a candlelight vigil was being held for Mrs. Linda Stevenson. Cars and trucks belonging to family and friends of the Stevensons crowded the parking lot. He thought back to all the accusations from Lloyd Stevenson since the very beginning. The detective questioned if there wasn't an ulterior motive for the man to place the blame on Melissa. Her attorney had pointed out Linda hired a private detective and what he discovered. Mr. Stevenson did have motive if he really was messing around with another woman, or women. He sure played up the part of the grief-stricken husband though. Larry had outright dismissed the idea when it had been brought up earlier. He even accused Melissa of hiring the detective to dig up dirt on Linda and her husband. While Jason didn't believe it for a second, Larry was adamant in his conviction. The private detective was scheduled to come in the next morning for questioning and to take a polygraph. Hopefully, they would get the answers they desperately needed then.

A few miles down the road, Jason found himself in the Stevenson's neighborhood. Not even knowing why, he parked his truck a few yards away from the house. He got out of the truck and took a good look around. Everything looked normal in the front. There was one car in the driveway – Linda's almost new metallic silver Lexus ES sedan. No one appeared to be home. Jason walked around the back of the house. The detective had no idea what he was looking for, but gut instinct told him to keep searching. Sure enough, at the back right corner of the house a window was open with a white linen curtain fluttering through the open slit. Kill Devil Hills was a quiet town, but still no one would leave a window open, especially during tourist season.

His police training kicked in as he quietly approached the open window with his 9mm pistol drawn. Listening intently, he heard at least one person moving around inside the house. Deciding against barging into the Stevenson home, Jason waited for the intruder to leave. It wasn't too long before a long, lanky leg appeared over the window sill. The cop reached out and grabbed the unsuspecting appendage and pulled the entire body out the window. When he saw who lay on the ground, Jason was astounded. Sprawled on the patchy grass, dressed in gym shorts and a Carolina Panthers t-shirt with a look of surprise and fear, was Melissa's teenage nephew, Logan Jones!

Jason lowered his weapon that had been pointed directly at the intruder. Flabbergasted, he shook his head. Considering he'd just caught Melissa's own nephew breaking into the victim's house, it did not help Melissa's case. "Can this day get any worse?" the weary cop thought to himself. Out loud he asked, "Logan, what in the bloody pit of Hades are you doing here?"

Just recovered from his shock at being caught in the act, Logan tried to plead his case. According to the young man, it was obvious the police were not going to even attempt to find the real killer. They were content they had arrested Aunt Mel. Based on those 'facts', he determined to find the killer himself. Logan refused to sit by while his aunt went to jail for something she most definitely did not do. He admitted to overhearing a conversation earlier that day between Melissa and her lawyer. They had discussed how Mr. Stevenson had been found out to be cheating on his wife and had taken out a large insurance policy on her life. It was clear to him that Mr. Stevenson killed his wife. It was obvious he wanted to peg Aunt Mel as a scapegoat with all his blustering about the discord between the two women. Logan wondered why the police hadn't already concluded the same. Therefore, he believed the cops simply didn't care about real justice being served as long as somebody, anybody paid the price. That somebody was his aunt!

Jason shook his head in disbelief. The poor kid! His love for her clouded his judgment and made him act out irrationally in order to vindicate her name. Quite frankly, the detective also wanted to prove her innocence. He just lacked the evidence to do so. He never wanted the guilt of sending someone to jail who wasn't guilty of the crime, especially if the death penalty could come into play. As he towered over the young man, Jason reached out his hand to help the lad up. "Ok, son. I believe you, but you do realize that by breaking into the Stevenson's house you committed a crime. This is not going to help your aunt's case."

Logan pleaded with Jason not to arrest him. He hadn't taken anything. Nothing was broken. The cop looked at him skeptically. "Okay, I didn't take anything per se. However, I did take a couple pictures with my phone," he grudgingly admitted. Without waiting for the inevitable question, he took out the phone to show Jason the images he captured. One was the high school picture Britney had also seen with Aunt Mel's face crossed out in red ink. Another was the Outer Banks Regional Bake-Off entry form that showed Linda intended to submit a Rosemary Sea Salt bread, which was his Aunt Mel's specialty. Everyone in town and beyond knew of Melissa's Rosemary Sea Salt bread, as well as a number of others. This particular bread was her landmark recipe. "Why would Mrs. Stevenson enter that particular type of artisan bread," he asked the cop, although he didn't expect an answer.

Jason informed Logan that they had known about the contest and the proposed bread entry. What he found to be unusual though was the form was pre-dated several weeks ago, as soon as the contest had been announced. However, the form had not been submitted yet. Against his better cop judgment, Jason decided to not haul Logan to the police station. Instead he told the boy to hop into his truck so they could get out of there before someone else saw them.

He drove to The Surf Shack where he bought a couple bottles of Orange soda and sat at the picnic table listening to the waves crash against the shore. The two men put their heads together to try to make some sense of this entire fiasco. Neither believed in Melissa's guilt. Both believed Mr. Stevenson may have something to do with his wife's murder, but again there was no evidence. Just speculation based on the findings of the private detective. If Melissa truly wasn't guilty, then someone certainly tried to make it look as if she were. That someone needed access to her home and her business.

They kept coming back to the same question. Why was Linda Stevenson inside the Kill Devil Delicacies bakery in the first place? Mr. Stevenson said that Melissa had asked Linda to meet her there after hours that evening. Melissa denied that accusation. It could be proved once forensics finished evaluating her phone's call log.

Mrs. Stevenson intended to enter the same type of bread as her rival, even though Melissa was famous for that particular recipe. Linda had no expertise in bread-making, only wedding cakes. Perhaps Mrs. Stevenson broke into the bakery to steal the recipe? It was an easy assumption given the circumstances. Maybe she told her husband that Melissa asked to meet her as an excuse so he wouldn't suspect what she was up to? Perhaps she didn't tell him anything and he made the whole thing up? What if he followed her to the bakery? What if someone else had found her there?

This list of questions grew exponentially by the minute. However, Jason realized it was getting late and he instructed Logan to call Maria and Luis to pick him up, since he was supposed to be in their care. Jason didn't want to risk taking the boy home himself.  If a news crew reported one of the detectives on the case was seen with the suspect's nephew; well then the chief of police would throw him off the case in a second. Then he wouldn't be able to help Melissa. Jason ensured Logan that he wasn't done making sense of all that had transpired and that he'd work to prove Mel's innocence.

Jason continued to drive around town into the night, thinking and pondering on how to find the true murderer. Then in the early morning hours a plan formulated in his head as he drove home for a quick shower and a short nap before putting it into action.

## Chapter 18

Melissa hadn't slept all night. The jail cell was tiny but neat. She had not seen or heard cockroaches roaming around during the night. From her standpoint, that was the highlight of her stay. Janice arrived early in the morning with a fresh change of clothes and her toiletries. Her nephew tagged along with her attorney. He looked like he hadn't slept in days. Her closest friends – Maria, Luis, and Cheryl – also showed up to support her at her bail hearing.

If the whole situation wasn't so dire, the whole thing would seem downright comical. Her? A lonely 44 year old widow and aspiring baker spent last night in jail for murder?! It was a nightmare!

With dark bags under her large, almond-shaped hazel eyes and her damp hair pulled back in a ponytail, Melissa emerged from her cell. She tried to smile but just couldn't pull it off. The guard escorted her back to the interrogation room where Jason was waiting. He looked weary as well, but there was something else about him she couldn't place at the moment. Surprisingly, the detective asked the others to join them in the room for a few moments before heading across the street to the courthouse.  It wasn't until after Jason finished explaining his plan to the group that Melissa realized, that look in his eyes was determination and excitement. It felt really good to know that he believed in her innocence and intended to prove it. She doubted his partner was aware of the plan or would like it if he knew. Yes, she was sure Detective "Grumpy" Reynolds would be dead-set against it.

The group walked solemnly over to the courthouse with Jason formally escorting the prisoner. Melissa's heart pounded loud and fast. She hoped her small endeavor into the drama club in high school helped her play her part now.

The bail hearing went rather smoothly until Detective Reynolds burst into the courtroom. Apparently, someone had told him the wrong time for the hearing. He was out of breath and red-faced. Jason didn't appear too happy with the arrival of his partner. With the look Larry gave him, Melissa suspected Jason had told him the wrong time. Not a good start for the plan to prove her innocence.

Despite the loud harrumphing from the older police officer and a few weak arguments by the assistant district attorney, the judge granted Melissa to be released on her own recognizance. Sweeter words had never been heard, at least not in the last week. Jason ushered her back to the precinct to pick up her things. Luis offered to drive her and Logan home. After congratulations from the others, they parted supposedly separate ways with Jason declaring he had a lot of paper work to catch up on. He gave her a sly wink as he turned back to his desk and she walked out the front door. As the door was closing behind her, Melissa heard the distinctly angry blustering of Detective Reynolds. For the first time in a while, she felt a genuine smile turn up the corners of her mouth. Logan barely contained his glee at the detective's bad mood.

Melissa hoped Jason's plan worked and his surly partner would be the one to leak the false information he intended to let spill. After dropping her off at home, the others went to fulfill their roles as well. There was nothing left for Melissa and Logan to do now but wait for nightfall.

## Chapter 19

After some rest and a decent meal, Melissa felt recovered enough to pull off her end of the plan. Actually, she was excited about it. Her heart thudded in her chest and she felt…alive. More alive than she had in a long time, probably since Kevin's death. Sometimes she really thought her heart had stopped and had died along with her husband after his plane crash. Today though, her heart somersaulted in her chest and adrenaline pumped through her entire body.

During the day, Jason filled his partner in on some "new information" he obtained overnight. His "source" stated that evidence had been overlooked at the bakery. This evidence, however, exonerated Mrs. Maples entirely. It could be found in the bakery office, but would not be easy to locate. He also informed Larry that the crime lab determined that one of the smudged fingerprints obtained did not belong to Melissa or anyone else associated with the bakery. It also didn't belong to Mrs. Stevenson. The lab claimed they lacked sufficient resources to get back out to the bakery until the following day to perform a thorough search for fingerprints that matched the smudged one. Additionally, they extracted a partial fingerprint from the bloodied cheese knife that matched the other smudged print. According to the forensics department, someone else had been in the bakery and had at some point held the suspected murder weapon. That someone wasn't Mrs. Maples.

Larry seemed more than a little skeptical with the news. Jason found it rather odd when the older cop hurried off to his desk to make a phone call immediately after being given this news. However, it was what he expected. After he wrapped up his call, Larry made a speedy retreat out to his car and left on "an errand". Jason took the opportunity to check his partner's desk phone to view the call log. The last outgoing number belonged to Lloyd Stevenson.

In the meantime, Melissa had been sworn to complete silence on the matter. She wasn't even allowed to tell Britney the truth. That was difficult since the young woman ran over to Melissa's house as soon as she heard about the outcome of the bail hearing. She was as vivacious as on any given normal day, but today Britney acted as if she had consumed five large espressos and an entire baker's dozen of donuts. She was hyped up. Neither Melissa nor Logan had ever witnessed her in this state. Playing out his part in the charade, Logan told her the fabricated tale of the additional evidence at the bakery, as well as the fingerprints. They both hated lying to the woman, but Jason firmly held that the story had to remain the same in each telling and re-telling for the plan to work. Melissa chalked up Britney's agitation to being nervous about working with a possible killer or losing her job if her boss gets thrown in prison for the rest of her life. Perhaps she was sensitive to what her socialite boyfriend and his family would say about her working for a murderer.

Luis, Maria, and Cheryl carried out their end of the bargain. They repeated the same story to just about everyone who came into their shops. It made for quite the gossip and spread just as fast. By noon, even the tourists were well acquainted with the tale.

Later that evening, the streets of downtown Kill Devil Hills were quiet. The only light came from a flickering lamp post. Melissa insisted Logan stay home, but the boy wasn't very good at following orders. He promised to stay out of sight, but he fully intended to be there to watch over his Aunt Mel.

The police tape still remained around the back door, but this time Melissa ignored it completely. She entered the building using a small flashlight to see where she was going. She made her way to the office. She planned to wait there until an 'expected' visitor arrived. If no one did, then the plan failed and she really faced jail time. The determined baker refused to go down without a fight though. Her life and her freedom were at stake. Besides, Jason was so certain the plan would work.

It wasn't until after the town clock tower struck 1:00 a.m. that Melissa heard the creaking of the back door as it swung on its rusty hinges. Her heart pumped so loudly in her chest she was sure whoever was there heard it. "Oh my! It worked! It really worked!" she thought with barely contained excitement. Footsteps came closer and closer to where she was hiding in the office, behind the tall metal file cabinet. Logan had stuffed his lanky legs into one of the cabinets under the cash register to stay out of sight, especially since he wasn't even supposed to be there. Moments later, the office door knob rattled as someone turned it to gain access to the room. Once the door clicked shut again, the interior lights switched on almost uncovering her hiding spot in the corner. She thanked her lucky stars she had the foresight to pile up boxes along the file cabinet to further conceal her.

She overheard drawers open and close. Items in and on the desk were shuffled around. Books and knick-knacks on the bookcase clattered as they were knocked over. Melissa peeked out from her hiding spot. She saw the backside of a man, not quite six feet tall with broad shoulders and an athletic build. Definitely, not Lloyd Stevenson. He wore dark clothes and latex gloves covered his large hands. When the man turned around, she clamped her hand over her mouth to keep from gasping in shock. A mere three feet away stood Eddie Johnson Jr., Britney's boyfriend!

Just as Eddie was within inches of discovering her, the office door banged open. Jason charged into the tiny room with his pistol drawn and shouted, "Police! Hands up!" The weathered cop looked more than a bit surprised to find the young man standing in the office. By the expression on Eddie's face, he was shocked to be discovered. However, he quickly did as he was told. Just a few moments later, another cop entered pushing Britney into the office with her hands already cuffed behind her back. He found her waiting outside in Eddie's prized Audi. Jason cuffed Eddie. The cops moved the suspects to the outer room to await a squad car to take them to the station.

Clearly, Eddie seemed bewildered and lost. The spoiled rich kid recovered quickly enough and demanded his lawyer. He also issued threats to the police. "Don't you KNOW who my father is?" he repeated over and over. Melissa wasn't a cop or a lawyer, but she was fairly certain his father wouldn't be able to get little Eddie out of this scrap. He eventually fell silent as he realized his proclamations were for naught.

Jason came back into the office to inform Melissa it was over. As she walked out to face Britney and Eddie, she heard the scraping of wood as Logan extracted himself from his own hiding place. The look on the cops' faces were clear. They were not happy the minor nephew tagged along for this adventure.

Melissa saw the horror on Britney's face as reality dawned on the young woman. The other officer read them their Miranda rights when she blurted out the whole sordid story. Jason stopped her and asked if she really wanted to talk without a lawyer present. Eddie muttered under his breath for her to "Shut up". As tears streamed down her face, Britney shook her head 'yes'.

The story she told was stranger than even the one that suggested Melissa was a murderer. Based on the severe facial expressions from Eddie, there was little doubt as to the truth of her tale. The night in question, Britney left the bakery to take the proceeds to the night bank depository. Eddie planned to pick her up a little while later for a big party at the golf club in Kitty Hawk. It wasn't until she was already at her small rental house that she realized she left her cell phone and personal wallet at the bakery. Using her roommate's phone, she called Eddie to ask him to swing by the bakery and pick the items up. Although aggravated at the request, he agreed.

At this point, Eddie saw no point in remaining quiet so he added to the tale. When he arrived at the Kill Devil Delicacies that night to retrieve Britney's things, the back door was wide open. He suspected Melissa was still inside so he walked right in. Instead, he found Linda Stevenson turning the place upside down. Pots and pans covered the counters and floors. The woman appeared near wild as she frantically tried to unlock the office door. At first, she didn't even realize she was no longer alone. He called her name a few times. Still she didn't respond at all. Finally, he grabbed her from behind. The wild look in her eyes as she turned around terrified him.

According to Eddie, the woman struggled to get away and fought him like an alley cat. He was certain he should keep her there until he could call the cops to pick up the intruder. She managed to knock him over the head with a large blunt serving spoon. The injured young man shoved her away from him. This gave her an opportunity to grab some sort of knife laying on the counter. He couldn't tell what type of knife. It all happened so fast. Mrs. Stevenson slashed at him with the knife. He overpowered her and grabbed the wrist of the hand holding the cooking item, now turned weapon. She thrashed around some more. Not even sure how it happened, Eddie claimed that in the scuffle he brought her arm up behind her head. She tried to jerk away from his grasp but instead the movement backfired. Instead of freeing herself, the motion caused the blade to puncture the back of her neck, just below her head.

Melissa inwardly cringed at the young man's description of Linda's death. Britney filled in the rest of the story. Eddie had called her in a panic at home. She literally ran the five blocks to the bakery and found him cowering in the corner with Linda's dead body bleeding out in the middle of the room. His large body shook uncontrollably and he whimpered something about what his daddy would do to him if he found out.

The young woman credited her "street smarts" with being able to manage the situation. She got Eddie out of there quickly. As he calmed down at her place, she went back to clean up any evidence of either of them being there. Almost as an afterthought, she attempted to make the scene look like a robbery. With a guilty look, she revealed to Melissa that she had watched her open the office door enough to figure out the security code. She also had found the safe late one night when she had been desperate for cash to pay off a bookie. There had been a number of times she had broken into the safe to abscond with cash. The repentant woman begged her to believe that she always put the money back as quickly as possible.

Britney swore that she never intended for Melissa to be suspected of the crime. However, Eddie believed that the police would figure it out eventually and come after him. The two decided, after Britney's snooping escapade at the Stevenson's house, that it would be easy to make it look like a long-held rivalry turned deadly. Before the cops brought Britney in for questioning, the two conspirators agreed to plant evidence to make it look even more like Melissa committed the crime. She planted the evidence at Melissa's home when she and Logan had gone back to the bakery. Eddie planted the bloodied knife at the bakery later that day. When they heard about new evidence at the bakery, the duo knew they had to find it before the cops or their whole plan would backfire. Britney claimed repeatedly that she never dreamed it was enough to have her boss arrested. The young woman cried as she apologized and begged her boss to trust her.

Logan started to tell her where she could take her apology, but Melissa held up a hand to shush the young man. She walked over to stand directly in front of Britney. She appeared calm, but rage burned in her heart and flashed in her eyes. Jason was concerned that she would strike Britney or the now stoically silent Eddie. Not that they didn't deserve it, but it could cause legal issues for the case. Instead, she glared at her once valued employee of the past three years and simply stated, "You're fired."

## Chapter 20

Before she knew it, summer was at an end. The last few weeks had flown by in a blur. Melissa's brother would drive up next weekend to pick up Logan for school. She was really going to miss that young man. Having him visit was the highlight of her year. This year in particular she had really needed him. Logan had kept her focused and determined throughout that entire ordeal after Linda Stevenson's death. It was due to Logan that she had fought as hard as she did for her freedom and the truth.

A lot had happened that summer. Eddie was arrested and charged with manslaughter. His father hired a team of high-priced attorneys to keep the young heir out of prison. Britney pled guilty to obstruction of justice and evidence tampering. She was sentenced to three years of community service at the local YMCA and probation for another 18 months after that. The young woman actually had the gall to come by the bakery one day to beg for her job back. Melissa slammed the door in her face.

The surly Detective Reynolds never apologized for his treatment of her. He begrudgingly admitted he was wrong, but argued that anyone could have made that mistake. However, the end of the case left him free to finally retire. With a nice gold commemorative watch and a letter of thanks, Larry Reynolds left the force and Kill Devil Hills. He and his wife moved to Augusta, Georgia, to be closer to their grandchildren. Melissa admitted she would absolutely NOT miss him.

Mr. Stevenson issued a written letter of apology to Melissa, after hearing from Janice Littleton, Attorney at Law. Melissa never considered suing him for slander, as her lawyer advised. She secretly didn't mind Janice ruffling his feathers a little though. The man was just happy the life insurance policy paid out. It took him all of one week to sell Linda's bakery to one of her assistants, put his house up for sale, and move to Miami with his new lady love – the leggy blonde from the strip club. His children were no longer speaking to him.

As the cool Atlantic Ocean lapped at her feet, she watched Logan trying to teach his new female friend Emily how to surf. She was the granddaughter of one her best clients, Mrs. Hawkins. The woman's appetite for Melissa's lemon-sage bread probably accounted for a few added pounds over the last year to her husband and herself. Emily, however, was smart and beautiful with long flowing blonde hair and a spattering of freckles over her nose. The two teenagers together were an adorable couple.

Melissa smiled thoughtfully. It was easy to see the two liked each other as more than friends, but they kept their budding relationship low key. With Logan returning to Charlotte and Emily headed back to Fairfax, Virginia, the two were mature enough to realize a long distance romance at their early age would be too difficult to maintain. Her nephew discussed his emergent feelings with his aunt over the course of the summer. She spent many a late night listening to him go on and on about Emily. Aunt Mel was thrilled to be the young man's confidante. Young, innocent love was truly grand.

Laughing as she watched Emily fall off her board and into the arms of her teacher, Melissa felt a strong, tan arm surround her waist. She didn't flinch. Instead, she placed her hand over Jason's and leaned back into his muscular chest with a contented sigh. Never in a million years would she have believed that she could have feelings for a man other than Kevin. When he died, she truly imagined that all love had died with him.

Shortly after the conclusion of the case, there had been a knock on her door. When she opened it, she was greeted by an enormous bouquet of sunflowers. Hiding behind the flowers had been the detective that had helped clear her name and kept her out of jail. She tried to thank him a number of times. He decided that she could thank him by going to dinner with him, at least once. Well, that had been many dinners ago. Melissa and Jason had been near inseparable all summer. Best of all, Logan and Jason had become fast friends as well. If not with their respective lady friends, the two boys were fishing or surfing together. With the young man leaving soon, Jason threatened to make Melissa go fishing with him until next summer. She agreed, as long as she didn't have to touch any bait.

Yes, the summer had been eventful in more ways than one. Although it started out horrific, Melissa didn't regret a second of it. Because of the ordeal, she felt stronger than she had in years. The last few years alone had taken its toll. Now she enthusiastically embraced life anew. With her business booming, an upcoming guest spot on a nationally televised cooking show – thanks to her easy first place win at the Outer Banks Regional Bake-Off with her famous Rosemary Sea Salt bread – and a new man in her life, Melissa was indeed happier than she had been in years. Watching the young lovebirds splashing in the ocean, she smiled and knew that life had just begun again.

# Your Free Gift

I wanted to show my appreciation for supporting my work so I've put together a Bonus Chapter for you. Just visit the link below:

http://outerbanks1_freegift.gr8.com/

Thanks!

Phoebe T. Eggli

Timber Publishing

## Sample Chapter from Book 2 of the Outer Banks Baker Mystery Series

**Sage Advice to Cover Up a Murder**

**Chapter 1**

Situated just south of Kill Devil Hills, NC, Oregon Inlet served to separate the more bustling northern Outer Banks communities from the small barrier islands. A massive hurricane in 1846 created the inlet - a new body of water between Bodie Island and Pea Island. The "Oregon" a ship trapped in the Pamlico Sound during the storm, witnessed the rift-causing event. Thus, the name. This spot had been well-known for ages as the prime fishing spot for any avid fisherman or woman.

William Hawkins spent what seemed to be his entire life with Johnson Shipping International. Now, at age 62, he finally realized his dream…to fish. Anytime, anywhere. He would no longer be a victim of the white-collar meat-grinder. His wife was none too happy with his abrupt early retirement. Frankly, he no longer cared what she wanted. As far as he was concerned, tonight was the most exciting day of his life. No meetings. No status reports due. No finding new ways to cover up details of dirty deals for Mr. Edward Johnson, Sr. No, today was wide open. Nothing for him to do but breathe in the salt air off the Atlantic Ocean as he repeatedly cast his large surf rod and reel into the waters of Oregon Inlet. William meant to spend as much as his retirement right here with a fishing rod in one hand and a bottle of Coors in the other. Most importantly, he meant to spend as much time away from his nagging wife of 40 years.

As the sun descended over the infamous North Carolina dunes, William unloaded his old light blue '72 Chevrolet C20 truck. He had everything he needed for an entire night's worth of fishing:

- One rod and reel
- Full tackle box with all the essentials for surf fishing
- Cooler full of beer and water bottles, with plenty of bait wedged in
- Italian sub on wheat bread with chips from the local bait and sandwich shop
- Extra jacket if the breeze off the ocean got too chilly
- Loaf of lemon sage bread still wrapped in the decorative paper from the Kill Devil Delicacies bakery to snack on

- Beach chair with cup holder
- Camp lanterns and a large flashlight
- Large fish net
- Cell phone (turned off)

Yes, William was set for his first perfect night as a retiree.

Hours later, as the sun began to rise again over the Atlantic Ocean, Logan slowed his scooter down as it traversed the pavement onto the sandy beach of Oregon Inlet. The place was mostly deserted, except for an ancient looking truck parked further out, closer to the rocks bordering the bridge. The young teen didn't see anyone around though. Whoever owned the truck must be nearby as a ragged beach chair was still embedded in the sand, despite the tide threatening to engulf it.

Before unloading his own fishing gear from the small compartment on the back of the scooter, Logan attempted to rescue the chair before it was washed away by the waves. As he moved the chair back to higher ground, he looked around for the truck's occupant. "It's probably some dude passed out after a night of fishing and drinking," he thought as he approached the Chevy. This spot was known for night fishing, but his aunt never allowed him to fish alone at night. Mostly because she knew it was common for night fisherman to bring plenty of alcohol to keep them company throughout the long hours until dawn. With his aunt's boyfriend working the night shift, Logan had to wait for morning.

As the teenaged boy turned the corner of the truck, he discovered an elderly man lying unconscious in the sand. He ran over to check if the man was okay. Logan noticed the awkward position of the man's body, as if he had fallen from the tailgate of the truck over the side. He kneeled beside the white-haired man and shook him slightly in an attempt to wake him. Unsuccessful, the boy worried that the man was seriously injured or had a heart attack. Intending to attempt CPR, he checked for a pulse and leaned over to listen to his chest for a heartbeat. No pulse, no heartbeat, no breath. The man was already cold to the touch.

In a panic, Logan grabbed a cell phone that was clutched in the dead man's hand. He dialed 911. After he relayed all the information to the 911 operator and waited for the paramedics to arrive, the frightened young man thought back to last summer. To say it had been eventful would be an understatement. At the start of his summer vacation, he discovered the dead body of Mrs. Stevenson in his Aunt Mel's bakery – the Kill Devil Delicacies. It had not taken long to prove his aunt didn't kill the woman, but the event had cast a damper over the start of his summer. The majority of the season had been salvaged once they discovered the real killer. Although he admitted it had added excitement to his vacation, he had hoped that this summer would be less dramatic. Sadly, Logan's summer was about to get much worse.

## Recipes:

### Rosemary Sea Salt Bread

Ingredients:

> 4 Cups Flour
> 2 ¼ Cups Water
> 2 tsp Salt
> ¼ tsp Dry Active Yeast
> 2 Tbsp. Fresh Rosemary Chopped Finely or 1 Tbsp. Dry Rosemary Flakes
> 1 Tbsp. Coarse Sea Salt – Sprinkled on top of bread at time of baking
> Cornmeal - Sprinkled in the Dutch oven – not mixed in dry the ingredients

Instructions:

Mix flour, salt and yeast in a large mixing bowl. If using Dry Rosemary Flakes then mix them in the dry ingredients. Or if you're using Fresh Rosemary then mix it with the water and allow it to soak in the water for at least 5 minutes to allow the flavor to spread through the water. Then pour and mix the wet ingredients into and with the dry ingredients. Stir until ingredients are well mixed. Dough may seem extra moist, which is perfectly normal. Then cover the bowl and allow to sit at room temperature for 12-18 hours.

Preheat the oven to 500ºF with a cast iron Dutch oven or Le Creuset style enameled pot in the oven preheating as well.   Once the oven and Dutch oven has been preheated, pull the Dutch oven out of the oven and remove the lid.  Then sprinkle some cornmeal in the bottom of the Dutch oven.  On a lightly floured surface pour out the dough, form into a ball, and place inside of the Dutch oven.  At this point sprinkle the Coarse Sea Salt over the top of the bread.  Replace the Dutch oven lid and place the Dutch oven in the oven.  Bake for 30 minutes, then remove the lid and continue to bake for 8-15 minutes, depending on how brown you want the crust to be.

Note:  If you don't have 12-18 hours to allow the dough to rest, you may increase the amount of yeast to 1 tsp and only wait 6 hours before baking the dough.  However, the longer you weight, the more sourdough-like the bread will be.

The trick to this bread is allowing it to rest for the 12-18 hours and its high moisture content, which turns to steam while being baked with the lid on the Dutch oven.  Once we remove the Dutch oven lid, then we begin to bake the outside for a nice crispy crust!

## Cranberry Orange Bread

Ingredients:

> 4 Cups Flour
> 2 ¼ Cups Water
> 2 tsp Salt
> ¼ tsp Dry Active Yeast
> Heaping ½ Cup of Craisins
> 2 Tbsp. Orange Zest
> Cornmeal - Sprinkled in the Dutch oven – not mixed in dry the ingredients

Instructions:

Mix flour, salt and yeast in a large mixing bowl. In another small bowl mix craisins, orange zest, and water. Allow them to soak in the water for at least 5 minutes to allow the flavors to spread through the water. Then pour and mix the wet ingredients into and with the dry ingredients. Stir until ingredients are well mixed. Dough may seem extra moist, which is perfectly normal. Then cover the bowl and allow to sit at room temperature for 12-18 hours.

Preheat the oven to 500ºF with a cast iron Dutch oven or Le Creuset style enameled pot in the oven preheating as well. Once the oven and Dutch oven has been preheated, pull the Dutch oven out of the oven and remove the lid. Then sprinkle some cornmeal in the bottom of the Dutch oven.  On a lightly floured surface pour out the dough, form into a ball, and place inside of the Dutch oven.  Replace the Dutch oven lid and place the Dutch oven in the oven.  Bake for 30 minutes, then remove the lid and continue to bake for 8-15 minutes, depending on how brown you want the crust to be.

Note:  If you don't have 12-18 hours to allow the dough to rest, you may increase the amount of yeast to 1 tsp and only wait 6 hours before baking the dough.  However, the longer you weight, the more sourdough-like the bread will be.

The trick to this bread is allowing it to rest for the 12-18 hours and its high moisture content, which turns to steam while being baked with the lid on the Dutch oven.  Once we remove the Dutch oven lid, then we begin to bake the outside for a nice crispy crust!

## Cheryl's Bacon Potato Cheddar Soup

Ingredients:

6 Potatoes
1 Onion
3 Carrots
3 Celery Stalks
2 Quarts (8 Cups) Chicken or Vegetable Broth
1 Cup Milk
½ Cup Cream
½ tsp Salt (or more to taste)
½ tsp Pepper
½ tsp Cajon Seasoning
3 Tbsp. Flour
1 Cup Sharp Cheddar Grated
6 Bacon slices, sliced into thin strips and
cooked, while saving some bacon grease
Minced Parsley – to garnish
Additional Grated cheese – to garnish

Instructions:

Cook and set aside the bacon and bacon grease ahead
of time. Place some of the grease in the bottom of the
large soup pot you'll be using for the soap. Finely
dice the onion, carrots, and celery and place them in
the pot. Over medium heat cook these ingredients for
2-3 minutes. Then add peeled and diced potatoes and
continue cooking for an additional 5 minutes. At this

point you can add the salt, pepper, and Cajun seasoning. Then add the broth and continue cooking for an additional 10 minutes, or until the potatoes start to feel tender. Then in another small bowl, mix milk and flour. Once mixed pour milk and flour mixture into the soup and allow it to cook for an additional 5 minutes. At this point you can choose to remove some of the soup to be blended for a smoother soup. It's suggested that you remove 2/3 of the soup to be blended. Use caution when blending the soup, and ideally do so once the soup has been allowed to cool. Once the soup is blended add it back to the soup pot and bring back up to heat. Then add the 1 Cup of Cheddar cheese and mix thoroughly. Then add the cream. At this point you can add the bacon pieces or wait and use them to garnish. You can now serve the soup and garnish with parsley, more cheese, and/or bacon pieces.

**Now take it to your dearest friend who may be experiencing a difficulty in his/her life.**
**This soup is particularly useful when a friend has recently been accused of murder!**

First Published, 2015

Timber Publishing
Oakley, UT 84055
www.timberpublishing.com

25623819R20101

Made in the USA
San Bernardino, CA
05 November 2015